P9-DWC-035

CAUGHT BETWEEN

A BULLET AND

A CANNONBALL

☆

Torn had no idea how one coaxed this big iron monster into motion, but he had a hunch this bizarre ambush was all about destroying the engine.

Precious seconds ticked away. Without conscious thought, he had marked the time between the first and second shots, and knew the third was due. In the cab, with his ear buffeted by the hiss of steam and huff of the boiler, he could not hear the lethal whistle of the shell, yet he sensed that this time it would strike square on.

Spinning, he hurled himself off the apron. A heartbeat later the boiler exploded in a ball of flame, and the force of the explosion flung him to the ground with such violence that the impact knocked him out.

Also by Hank Edwards

THE JUDGE

WAR CLOUDS

GUN GLORY

TEXAS FEUD

STEEL JUSTICE

LAWLESS LAND

BAD BLOOD

RIVER RAID

BORDER WAR

DEATH WARRANT

Published by
HARPERPAPERBACKS

ATTENTION: ORGANIZATIONS AND CORPORATIONS

Most HarperPaperbacks are available at special quantity
discounts for bulk purchases for sales promotions, premiums,
or fund-raising. For information, please call or write:
Special Markets Department, HarperCollins Publishers,
10 East 53rd Street, New York, N.Y. 10022.
Telephone: (212) 207-7528. Fax: (212) 207-7222.

THE JUDGE

IRON ROAD

Hank Edwards

HarperPaperbacks
A Division of HarperCollins*Publishers*

If you purchased this book without a cover, you should be aware that this book is stolen property. It was reported as "unsold and destroyed" to the publisher and neither the author nor the publisher has received any payment for this "stripped book."

This is a work of fiction. The characters, incidents, and dialogues are products of the author's imagination and are not to be construed as real. Any resemblance to actual events or persons, living or dead, is entirely coincidental.

HarperPaperbacks *A Division of* HarperCollins*Publishers*
10 East 53rd Street, New York, N.Y. 10022

Copyright © 1993 by HarperCollins*Publishers*
All rights reserved. No part of this book may be used or reproduced in any manner whatsoever without written permission of the publisher, except in the case of brief quotations embodied in critical articles and reviews. For information address HarperCollins*Publishers*,
10 East 53rd Street, New York, N.Y. 10022.

Cover illustration by Gabriele

First printing: December 1993

Printed in the United States of America

HarperPaperbacks and colophon are trademarks of HarperCollins*Publishers*

10 9 8 7 6 5 4 3 2 1

CHAPTER 1

THE RHYTHM OF THE WHEELS ON THE RAIL JOINTS LULLED Clay Torn to the very rim of sleep as the combination work and passenger train rolled down the iron road across the plains of southern Colorado.

Torn was a tall, lean man dressed in black. His wheat-colored hair was close-cropped. Clean-shaven, he was sun dark and not unhandsome. His eyes were a steel-cast gray. There was something grim and melancholy about the man. Something that kept others at a distance. Those who did not know him assumed he was a gambler or gunslinger. He was neither.

He shared a bench with a whiskey drummer who was careful to mind his own business. Torn's few belongings were in a small black leather valise shoved under the bench. His scabbarded Winchester 44/40 was strapped to the valise.

Though weary, Torn could not seem to drop off to sleep. A number of things conspired against him. For one, the car was crowded and stuffy. The old coal-burning stove in its rear was going full blast. It was the first day of April, but spring was tardy, and outside it was still winter cold. The heat from the stove, combined with the pungent aromas of wool and leather and unwashed bodies and stale tobacco smoke, served to produce an atmosphere Torn found claustrophobic.

Apart from that, Torn just did not much care for trains. His aversion could be traced back to a day fifteen years ago. On that day, Confederate Colonel Clayton Randall Torn had been loaded into a boxcar with a hundred other graycoat prisoners and sent down the B&O Railroad to a prisoner-of-war camp located at Point Lookout, Maryland. Torn had been captured by federal cavalry at the Battle of Gettysburg.

That train trip had been the beginning of sixteen months of pure living hell for Torn. From then on, he had been unable to set foot on a train without experiencing a cold shudder and an unpleasant, coppery taste in his mouth.

While he much preferred traveling alone on horseback, his job as a federal circuit judge for a district that included the Dakotas, Nebraska, Kansas, Missouri, and Arkansas sometimes required him to travel by rail. When trouble arose, he was dispatched to deal with it, and the frontier brand of trouble generally waited for no man.

Such was the case on this occasion. Normally Colorado was not his bailiwick, but this was a special assignment, with political overtones. That didn't bother him. Torn had no illusions about justice. Justice was his mistress, true enough, but she was fickle, and the handmaiden of politics.

General Orville Rhynes was the chief engineer for the Great Western Railroad. He also happened to be a crony of ex-President Ulysses S. Grant. Until recently, this had been an asset for Rhynes. Now, with Rutherford Hayes in the White House, it had the look of a liability.

As a result of the hotly disputed election that had taken place last year, Hayes owed some powerful men some big favors. Many of these men had Southern connections. It happened that the Great Western's chief rival, the Coastal & Northern Railroad, was run by Southern men. The election of Hayes had the appearance, at least, of promising great days ahead for the Coastal & Northern. At the same time it seemed to bode ill for the troubled Great Western.

"God knows how many gold and silver mines there are in those Colorado Rockies," General Rhynes had told Torn the day before in Dodge City. "The Great Western intends to push a spur through the high country to those mining camps. The prize is millions of dollars' worth of high-grade ore which needs to be freighted, and will be, on the first railroad that makes it through. The best and quickest way through is Wolf Creek Pass. We are in a race, sir, against the Coastal and Northern, to reach that pass first. There is room enough through that pass for only one railroad."

"Competition is the cornerstone of the free enterprise system," said Torn.

Rhynes gave him a funny look. "Honest competition, yes. But last year the Coastal and Northern beat us into the San Juan Valley and the only logical terminus of Durango. Know how they did it? By

hook and crook, Judge Torn. Their spies and saboteurs infiltrated our work crews. One disaster after
another befell us, and it was not just bad luck, as
some would have you believe."

"So you expect more of the same from the Coastal
and Northern this season."

"Absolutely." Rhynes was a blunt and brawny
man, with bushy sideburns framing a florid face,
which, now, turned an even more vivid crimson hue.
He rose from behind his desk and paced the office,
hands clasped behind his back. Though he had retired ten years earlier from the army, his military
bearing had not deserted him. "Those jackals with
the Coastal and Northern will stop at nothing. If they
whip us this year, the Great Western is finished. We
can expect no succor from the Hayes Administration. That much is certain."

"Where do I fit in?"

"We tried to handle it ourselves last year. Failed,
obviously. This season I wanted the power and authority of the federal government on our side."

"Did you ask for U.S. marshals?"

"I asked for a whole posse of U.S. marshals. They
sent one man instead. You. I suppose I shouldn't be
surprised. If Grant was still there . . . well, it would
be a different story."

"You believe I am just a token."

"To a degree, yes. But I've heard you have the gun
skills of a marshal. In addition, you have the power
not only to apprehend criminals, but also to bring
them to trial."

Torn's slate-gray eyes were hooded. If what General Rhynes claimed was so—if, in fact, the Coastal
& Northern had employed underhanded means to

compete with the Great Western—then indeed it would be a task tailor-made for his talents.

"That sounds like a tall job for one man," he said.

"There again, your appointment as a federal judge will stand you in good stead. You possess the authority to appoint as many men as you need to be deputy marshals."

"I'm allowed to choose these men?"

"Certainly. Handpick them, Colonel. Appoint them. And keep the Coastal and Northern honest. Give us a fair shot at Wolf Creek Pass."

Torn suppressed a smile. As with all military men, Rhynes subscribed to the notion that an officer was always an officer. Retired or active, it mattered not. The general remembered Torn from the war. They had served on opposite sides of that conflict. At Chancellorsville, Torn's South Carolina cavalry had slashed the regiment anchoring the extreme right of Rhynes's brigade to bloody ribbons.

To the general's credit, he held no grudge. He had put the war behind him. That he found himself turning to an ex-Confederate officer for help made no difference to him now. His attitude impressed Torn, who took an instant liking to the general. This was quite at odds with his expectations before the meeting with Rhynes. For while he had never met the Great Western's chief engineer, he had heard plenty about the man. Immediately after the war Rhynes had for a time served as a military governor in the defeated South, and his rule had been a harsh one.

"You must appear to be—and in fact you are—completely independent," continued the crusty old war-horse. "You may rely on Orly Bracken, the superintendent of construction, and Niles Keach, the man whom we have contracted for our iron. They will provide you with every assistance, but they are not to interfere with you in any way. Everything we have will be placed at your disposal. Your word will be law on the Great Western. You will answer to no one. Just get the job done."

"And what if I've been sent here by a hostile administration to make certain you fail?"

Rhynes grunted. "Not you. You wouldn't do that."

"No," said Torn gratefully. "I wouldn't."

"Just keep the Coastal and Northern on the straight and narrow, Judge Torn."

"That alone won't guarantee you'll win the race to Wolf Creek Pass."

"Of course not." Rhynes pounded fist into his hand. "All I'm asking for—all the Great Western requires—is a fair chance. Will you do everything in your power to see that we get at least that?"

"I will," promised Torn.

CHAPTER

2

As the train rolled on, Torn watched the sun set
in a blaze of fire-orange glory beyond the distant
blue line of snowcapped peaks. They paused briefly
at Alamosa. The end of the track lay about fifteen
miles farther west, near a place called Whiskey Flat.

The Great Western's railyard at Alamosa was a
beehive of activity, even at night. This was a major
staging area for supplies destined farther up the line.
Stacks of iron rails and wooden ties stood taller than
a two-story house on every side. "Moguls," as the
locomotives were called, huffed up and down the sid-
ings, jostling strings of cars to and fro. Men un-
loaded and loaded these cars, working by the light of
huge bonfires.

Torn's train was composed of two passenger cars,
five boxcars, and three flatcars. The two passenger
cars were hooked directly behind the Jupiter loco-

motive and its tender, and the eight cars behind them were loaded with stock and stores. Most of these were to be detached at Alamosa, so a one-hour stopover was scheduled.

Many of Torn's fellow passengers were disembarking here, but for every one that left, at least one came aboard. The night's wintery embrace invaded the car thanks to all this coming and going, and Torn was grateful for that—it helped clear his head.

He considered leaving the car, but was loath to surrender his seat. Bound for end-of-track, he did not want to go the rest of the way standing up, as it appeared many would have to do.

All manner of people were traveling on the iron road tonight. Aside from the men who worked on the railroad—the bridge crews and steel layers and graders—there were those who plied their trades in every end-of-track boomtown: cardsharps, gunslingers, drummers, doctors, lawyers, freighters, hunters.

Men of all descriptions flocked to places like Whiskey Flat—wild and woolly and usually wicked places. And when, next season, a new town sprang up farther down the line, most of them would go there, Whiskey Flat forgotten. Some young, some old, some honest, others not, they were all bound by a single desire: to have a piece of the action. It was the same, mused Torn, in the trail towns and the mining camps. The boomtown's life was short, burning bright and fierce like a fuse. Some would find what they wanted in Whiskey Flat. Others would lose everything they had to lose.

A man who found a place on a bench across the aisle drew Torn's attention. He was clad in fringed and beaded buckskin. Auburn hair was long to his shoulders. His face was bronzed and craggy, and his eyes like chips of blue ice. He carried a rifle in a sheath, which also sported fringe and exceptional Indian beadwork. Torn identified the weapon as a Sharps Big Fifty.

Hunters called the .50-90 the "Old Poison Slinger," and it was said that a man could hit a target at five miles with the rifle, though personally Torn thought he would wait to see such sharpshooting before he believed it. But there was no disputing that the Big Fifty rollingblock rifle was an outstanding firearm. Torn had no doubt that the colorful character across the aisle from him was a hunter.

More passengers piled into the car, and in short order all available seats were taken. The aisle began to fill. Torn was glad he had refrained from leaving the train during its Alamosa stop.

Then he saw the woman.

The first thing he noticed about her was her hair —black as a raven's wing—and his heart skipped a beat.

Melony Hancock's hair had been black like that.

He carried a daguerreotype in a pocket of his black frock coat. The photograph had been taken in a Charleston studio just before he had ridden off to war. Melony had been his fiancée, and as Shakespeare had said, parting was sweet sorrow, but he had promised to come back to her, and she had promised to wait, and given him the photograph to remember her by.

That day of parting he remembered still with excruciating clarity. It had been seventeen years since he had gone off to fight for the cause of Southern independence as an officer in a volunteer regiment of South Carolina cavalry. That day there had been flags flying and bands playing and crowds cheering, and war had seemed such a glorious enterprise. But it had been the last time he'd seen Melony, and countless times since he had cursed himself for having left her at all.

He had kept his promise. He had come back from the war, the survivor of a half-dozen major campaigns from Second Bull Run to Gettysburg, and sixteen months in a prisoner-of-war camp that most agreed had been the worst the federals had to offer.

Returning to South Carolina, he had found the Torn plantation, Ravenoak, in ruins, compliments of Sherman's invaders, and his family dead. And Melony gone. She, too, would have kept her promise, had she been able to. But Yankee deserters had abducted her, taking her with them in their flight to the frontier, and for all these years since, Torn had been searching.

So the woman's black hair sent his pulse racing, but that by now familiar disappointment followed quickly on the heels of hope, because she wasn't Melony. Torn had never seen this woman before. She was nearly as pretty as the woman captured in the daguerreotype Torn carried. She was delicate and pale and her eyes were an alluring smoky gray. There was a very demure, girlish quality about her.

Precisely because she was pretty she seemed out of place. There were women on the iron road, certainly. Some of the railroaders employed by the Great Western had wives. Those who didn't required occasional female companionship. So the calico queens flocked to end-of-track. One glance confirmed for Torn that this woman was not one of those women of easy virtue.

He had been brought up a gentleman, a member

of the landed gentry, a Southern aristocrat, and a dozen rough-and-tumble years on the frontier had not changed him much in that regard, at least where women were concerned. This one was looking for a place to sit, but there were no seats left, and she looked fatigued, so without second thought Torn was prepared to surrender his place for her.

The buckskin-clad hunter beat him to it.

Rising, he drawled, "Ma'am, I'd be obliged was you to take this here seat."

"Oh, no, I couldn't. . . ."

"You'd be doin' me an awful big favor," insisted the hunter. "Feels like I been sittin' here since the Great Flood, and these ol' long legs of mine are just plumb tired of it."

Torn smiled. The man had not been sitting five minutes.

The woman also smiled. "Oh, but I am certain I saw you, sir, in the depot only moments ago."

"Shucks," said the man, caught off guard. "I reckon you got me dead to rights, miss. But you'd still be doin' me a favor. I've spent more than twenty winters out on the plains or up in the mountains, and I just don't get very many chances to be a gentleman. I'd hate for this chance to get away from me. Please don't hold my truth stretchin' agin me."

"Oh, I shan't," she said, humor dancing in her eyes. "Thank you very much."

"Thank you," he said, stepping aside so that she could sit down with her little carpetbag in her lap.

Still more passengers boarded, until those in the aisle were packed like sardines. Torn seldom caught a glimpse of the woman through this wall of humanity. The car became overwarm and redolent with the human fragrance once more. Torn leaned his head back, closed his eyes, and sighed.

Eventually a steam whistle shrilled twice. A moment later the train lurched into motion.

Torn calculated it would take a half hour to reach Whiskey Flat. He tried to make himself as comfortable as possible and let the motion of the train and the song of the wheels on the rail joints lull him to sleep.

This time he dozed.

And then the steam whistle screamed again—a long shrill note, and the passenger car lurched against its couplings, lurched again. Men began to swear as those in the aisle were jolted off balance, and those on the benches were thrown violently about as the train came to a sudden stop.

Torn felt a blast of cold night air. A man on the bench behind him had muscled open a window and leaned out to see what he could see.

"Fire!" he yelped. "Big fire on the tracks up ahead!"

Pandemonium followed this announcement. Everyone started talking at once. More windows were thrown open, more men leaned out for a look. Others piled out of the car, front and rear.

Torn waited until the aisle had cleared somewhat before attempting to stand. While others lost their heads he had always been the type who remained calm and collected. He turned and bent to retrieve the Winchester 44/40. As he straightened the man in buckskins was right there in front of him.

"You must be Judge Torn."

"You have an advantage, sir. I don't believe I know you."

"Oh, we ain't never met," said the hunter. "My

name's Lewis Clark Gant. Folks call me Longshot, on account of they claim I'm a fair-to-middlin' shot with this here Leadslinger."

"You may get a chance to prove it before long," said Torn.

CHAPTER 3

"IF WE'VE NEVER MET," SAID TORN, "HOW IS IT THAT you know me?"

"I reckon it's more like I know about you. I seen that knife under your coat. Who else carries one like that?"

Torn nodded. In a custom-made shoulder rig that kept the weapon snug against the left side of his rib cage was a knife that had come to be as famous in its way as the man who owned it.

Once it had been a Chicopee saber, property of a Union sergeant assigned to the Point Lookout garrison. The sergeant, Karl Schmidt by name, had been a sadistic brute who devoted a great deal of his time and effort to the task of making Torn's incarceration sheer hell.

Schmidt had made it his personal mission to break Torn's spirit. He had failed, and the price of failure

14

had been death. In his escape from Point Lookout, Torn had killed Schmidt, using the saber. The blade had been with him ever since.

He had honed it down to its present fifteen inches of razor-sharp steel. It was easier to carry that way. While the Winchester 44/40 and the Colt Peacemaker were his principal weapons, the saber-knife, with its single guard bow intact, was an exotic ace-in-the-hole.

It, and the daguerreotype, were more than mere mementos. The photograph was a reminder of what he sought to find—Melony, and a piece of the life he had known before the war, the only happy time of his life. The saber-knife reminded him of his other obsession—to destroy animals like Karl Schmidt wherever they were to be found.

"You have sharp eyes," congratulated Torn.

"Reckon that's so. I was wonderin' whether you was a preacher or a gunhawk. I was leanin' toward gunhawk, seein' you sit there calm as all get-out with hell bustin' loose all around you."

"I've learned that a fight, if there's one in the making, will usually wait for me," said Torn, laconic.

Longshot smiled. "I like to know when I can count on a feller in a ruckus. I can tell you're one to ride the river with." He stuck out a hand. "And you can rely on me."

Torn shook the proffered hand. "You work for the Great Western?"

"Did last season. Bringin' in fresh meat for the railroad commissary. Wintered up in the high country, as usual. Hopin' they'll sign me on again this year."

"Excuse me."

It was the raven-haired woman.

"Could one of you tell me what is happening?"

"We don't know, ma'am," admitted Torn.

"But we'll find out," promised Longshot. "You just sit tight, little lady."

Torn and the hunter left the car. Most of the train's passengers were milling around on both sides of the track. The two men made their way forward to the Jupiter, where the engineer and fireman stood with several others, staring at the bonfire fifty yards up the iron road.

"They tore up two sections of rail," bemoaned the engineer.

Torn could see that this was so. The blaze lit up the night. Whoever had done the deed had used a pile of cross ties to start the fire and then thrown the rails on top. Sherman's federals had employed the same technique to destroy what remained of the Confederacy's railroad system during their march to the sea. After heating the rails, the bluecoats had bent them around tree trunks and telegraph poles, rendering them unsalvageable.

"We might as well go back to Alamosa," said the engineer. "Nothing else we can do. They'll have this stretch repaired tomorrow, and then we'll try again." He looked despondently at the fireman. "It's starting all over, ain't it?"

"Like last year?" queried Torn.

"Yep. Mister, I nearly got blowed up twice, and I rode one iron horse right off a bent rail. I'm beginning to think there are safer ways to make a living, and I am just about—"

A far-off sound cut him short. Everybody froze. Torn heard a whistling above the huff and hiss of the nearby locomotive. It was a familiar noise. It sent a tingle corkscrewing down his spine.

He had heard it last during the war.

But he couldn't believe it. He had to be mistaken. It made absolutely no sense, in this time and place.

Dumbfounded, arguing against his instincts, he stood there with the rest, a sitting duck.

The explosion, on the other side of the Jupiter mogul, was a blaze of fiery light and flame, a deafening percussion, a lot of acrid smoke.

"What the hell?" yelped the engineer.

"Cannon," said Torn.

They stared at him.

Another distant coughing sound, another whistling noise somewhere up in the inky-black night sky, and this time the exploding shell landed on their side of the train, a hundred yards away. Yelling men dived for cover or took off running in every direction.

"Jaysus!" hollered the fireman, white as a ghost, and took to his heels.

The engineer made as though to follow his colleague's example, but Torn grabbed his arm and detained him.

"You've got enough steam up to back the train out of here," said Torn.

"You're crazy."

"They're trying to find the range. They're going to blow the train to smithereens."

"Let 'em!" cried the railroader, struggling to get loose.

Torn released him. The man was thoroughly unnerved and completely useless.

He turned to Longshot. The hunter was standing his ground. In fact, the two of them seemed to be the only ones present who were capable of doing so. Torn doubted if Gant had ever been subjected to artillery fire before, but then some men just would not run.

As for Torn, a rigid calm overtook him. This cold disdain for danger had been forged in the crucible of battle—the direct result of enduring enemy fire and learning that there were no guarantees. The bullet and the cannonball did not discriminate between men who stood fast and those who ran away. The only thing a man could do was keep his head and behave in an honorable fashion. A soldier's only reward was knowing that if he fell, his comrades would remember that he perished bravely.

For the uninitiated, there was nothing in life so unsettling as an artillery bombardment, yet Longshot didn't even bat an eye, and Torn was impressed.

"Get everybody off the train," he told the hunter, "and clear of the tracks."

"The lady!" Longshot exclaimed, and headed for the first passenger car with long, loping strides.

Torn climbed aboard the Jupiter. He was not one to order someone else to do what he himself was not willing to try. Pausing there on the metal apron of the locomotive, he stared at the bewildering array of valves and pipes and levers decorating the face of the boiler. He had no idea how one coaxed this big iron monster into motion, but he had a hunch this bizarre ambush was all about destroying the engine. The tracks could be replaced in a matter of hours. The loss of the Jupiter would be a serious setback for the Great Western.

Precious seconds ticked away as Torn struggled to make sense of the engine's control mechanisms, and as he stepped forward to lay hand on a lever on the "four-dollar side" of the cab, he glanced left. Without conscious thought he had marked time between the first and second shots, and knew the third was due.

He saw a flicker of flame, and by its elevation surmised that the cannon stood on high ground—the backbone of a ridge south of the track and running parallel. In the cab, with his ear buffeted by the hiss of steam and huff of the boiler, he could not hear the lethal whistle of the shell as it hurtled through the air. Yet somehow he sensed that this time the gun crew would find their mark. This time the shell would strike the Jupiter square on.

Spinning, he hurled himself off the apron, and as he fell he heard the shell strike. A heartbeat later the boiler exploded in a ball of flame, and the force of the explosion flung him to the ground with such violence that the impact knocked him out.

4

WHEN TORN CAME TO, THE JUPITER MOGUL WAS A smoldering wreck of twisted, blackened iron. He was lying on the ground, on a blanket, covered by a greatcoat. The woman with the raven hair was sitting next to him, cloak pulled tight around her, her knees drawn up.

"Are you hurt?" he asked.

"No. But you are."

"I'm fine." Torn had a splitting headache. But it wasn't anything a good stiff shot of bourbon wouldn't cure.

"No broken bones, no bleeding, none that I could find, anyway," said Longshot as he hunkered down beside Torn. He handed over the Winchester 44/40. "Thought you might need this."

"Thanks." Torn checked his keywinder, found

that it had been smashed. Consulting the stars, he estimated the time of night.

"You've been out a couple hours," said the hunter. "You were lucky. I reckon the engine was what they were after. 'Cause when it went up, they stopped shooting."

Men were standing in clumps up and down the track. The cross-tie bonfire had burned down, and some stood around it, warming themselves.

"Anybody hurt?" asked Torn.

"No. Least I don't think so. Some unaccounted for. Engineer, for one, and a passel of Irishmen. Guess those paddies decided it wasn't healthy working for the Great Western."

"It isn't," said Torn, and got to his feet. His head reeled, and he swayed a bit, but managed to keep his balance.

The young fireman came up. He looked crestfallen. "You're Judge Torn," he said, and gestured at Longshot. "This feller told me. I'm ashamed of running off the way I did, Judge."

"Least you come back," said Longshot generously. "Which is more than I can say for your partner."

"Being shot at by a cannon does rattle you," said Torn. "Don't worry about it."

"A cannon," murmured Longshot, shaking his head in wonder. "Out here in the middle of nowhere? Beats all I ever seen, and I thought I'd seen the elephant."

"Twelve-pounder, would be my guess," said Torn.

"But where do you get a cannon way out here?" queried Longshot.

"One thing is certain," said Torn. "It'll be easy enough to track. If I only had a horse."

"You can borrow one of mine."

Torn stared at Longshot, surprised.

"I got me two of the fastest cayuses on the high plains, yonder in one of them boxcars," the buckskin-clad hunter explained. "Tools of my trade, you might say."

"I want to talk to you about that. Your trade, I mean."

"We can palaver on the trail," said Longshot. "Moon's on the rise. We don't need to wait for daylight. My eyes are pretty sharp, if I do say so myself."

"You've decided to come along, I take it."

"Didn't I say that? It's the condition for the loan of the horse."

"I'll accept that condition."

Longshot went to fetch his ponies.

"We're long overdue at Whiskey Flat," said the fireman. "I expect they'll send out a train to find out what happened to us."

Torn nodded, glanced at the woman. "You watch after her," he told the railroader. "If anything happens to her, you'd better start running again. And this time don't come back."

The young man gulped down a big lump in his throat. "Don't worry, Judge. I won't let nothing happen to her. I'll die 'fore anything happens to—"

"Pardon me," said the woman. "But I can take care of myself, Judge Torn."

"I'm afraid I didn't catch your name, ma'am."

"Rachel Bailey. You need not bind this young man to be my protector."

"Yes, ma'am. Then maybe you'll watch over him."

Shouldering the Winchester, Torn walked away, heading for the boxcars.

Longshot was bringing two horses down a freight

ramp. Torn looked them over with an experienced eye. Few men knew as much about horses. He had been raised among them—could, literally, ride before he had learned to walk. Ravenoak, the Torn plantation, had been famous throughout the Carolinas for the quality of its Thoroughbreds. And as a cavalry commander during the War Between the States, Torn had learned even more about horses under the most trying conditions.

Longshot's ponies were truly two of the finest Torn had seen in quite a while. They were Indian-bred, one a paint, the other an Appaloosa. The Palouse stood two hands taller than the paint, but apart from size there wasn't a thin dime's worth of difference between them. They both looked to be "long" horses, with plenty of spirit, and stamina to spare.

Torn drew the Palouse. He borrowed a storm lantern from the boxcar, and in short order he and Longshot had put the train behind them.

Reaching the top of the low ridge seven hundred yards south of the iron road, they combed the crest in the general vicinity of the cannon's previous position. As Longshot had predicted, moonlight bathed the plains in its silvery glow. Still, Torn employed the lantern, holding it down at stirrup level so that its mustard-yellow light would play to full advantage on the ground.

It didn't take them long to find what they were seeking. Cannon, with a crew of seven, the latter mounted, had headed south across the sagebrush plains. Torn and Longshot followed the sign.

They rode through the night, and by dawn it was obvious that they had gained ground on those whom they pursued. The plains were intersected by arroyos, some of which were difficult to negotiate with cannon and limber, and as a result Torn and Long-shot made the better time.

At daybreak they paused to give their mounts a rest. They cooked coffee over a buffalo-chip fire. "I just ain't worth spit iffen I don't get my java in the morning," confessed Longshot. Torn didn't begrudge him the slight delay. The men they were after weren't far ahead of them, and action was imminent. Torn wanted to have that palaver with Longshot Gant before the shooting started.

"You know who I am," prefaced Torn. "So you probably know what I'm here to do."

The hunter nodded. "To see that the Great Western gets a fair shake. That's a tall order, friend. The Coastal and Northern's owned by big-money men back east, but the man who runs the show out here's a feller named Ezra Stinson. The Coastal and Northern ain't the first railroad Stinson's been in charge of, and he has a reputation for gettin' the job done no matter what. He deserves that reputation. He don't let nothing and nobody stand in his way. He's forgotten more about railroadin' than most railroaders will ever know. He'll be a hard man to beat, Judge."

"The job they've given me is more than one man can handle," said Torn. "I have the authority to appoint men to help me. You're the kind of man I'm looking for. You'll be sworn in as a United States deputy marshal. You'll take orders from me, and when the job's done, the appointment will cease. You'll be paid a government wage, and in addition you'll get a bonus from the Great Western."

Longshot frowned. "I ain't cut out to be a lawman, Judge. I ain't never took orders from nobody. I'm used to livin' free and footloose. Reckon it's in my blood. My father came west with the Lewis and

Clark outfit." The hunter grinned. "He even named me after them two."

"Who gave you the nickname?"

"Blame the Shoshone for that business. Used to live with 'em. Fine people. Was out hunting one spring and bagged an elk at just over a mile with this here Leadslinger. They were awful impressed, I guess, and took to callin' me Longshot."

Torn sipped his coffee, trying to suppress disappointment at Gant's reluctance to sign on. "Well, there's liable to be some shooting today. If you want no part of it, I understand."

Longshot chuckled. "Oh, I didn't come along for the ride. I ain't opposed to fightin', so long as it's for a good cause. It rankles me some, I confess, that them Coastal and Northern coyotes don't mind shootin' at innocent folk just to kill a locomotive. They need a comeuppance."

"Then what is it about my offer you shy away from?"

"The part about being on a payroll. Let's leave it like this, Judge. I'll float my stick with yours and I won't swear to anything or take any government money, and I'll feel like I'm free to go my own way whenever the notion comes up on me. How's that suit you?"

"I guess I'll go along with it."

They finished their coffee, tightened cinches, and rode on.

Midmorning found them in a willow thicket on the banks of a shallow rocky river, gazing at a sod house on the other side, backed up against a hill and shaded by dusty gray cottonwoods. There were a dozen horses in a pole corral. All looked used up.

The cannon and limber stood in front of the soddy, and a sentry stood watch on the roof, a carbine cradled in his arms.

"I'll be damned," breathed Torn.

"What?" asked Longshot.

The lookout wore a butternut tunic with red collar and piping. Aside from that he wore typical Westerner garb. But the tunic was definitely Confederate issue.

"That man and I," said Torn, "used to fight on the same side."

"Make a difference today?" queried the hunter, watching Torn closely.

"No. This is another war entirely."

"Then let's start her up," said Longshot.

CHAPTER 5

"WE TRACKED SEVEN MEN," SAID LONGSHOT. "THERE'S one. Where do you reckon the other six are?"

"Inside, I hope," replied Torn. "They rode all night. It wasn't easy, hauling that gun across the plains. They've had their breakfast and I'd guess most of them have turned in for a little shut-eye."

"So if we can get shed of that lookout, we'd have a chance at gettin' the drop on the others."

They glanced at each other. Longshot grimaced.

"Oh, we could go chargin' over there like Custer," said the hunter, "and I could put that lookout under with a single shot, and we could be on the others like stink on a skunk 'fore they managed to get both eyes open. But I'd ruther not do it that way. Now, I won't try to tell you I ain't never kilt a man before, 'cause I have. But they've all been fair fights, and the men I done for had just as much chance as I did of walkin' away. Shootin' a feller from ambush just don't sit well with me, Judge."

"Me either," said Torn.

Longshot dismounted, handed reins and rifle to Torn.

"Then why don't you just sit tight, and I'll take care of that feller quietlike."

"Good luck."

Longshot vanished into the brush.

Torn settled down, expecting to have a long wait. He calculated it would take Longshot a good while to work his way around behind the soddy without being seen. But he never entertained a moment's doubt that the hunter could get the job done.

His keywinder broken, Torn could only estimate the passage of time, and he was sure more than an hour had passed before he saw Longshot again. He had a clear view of the sod house and the sentry from his place of concealment in the willows.

He figured Longshot would go downriver a good piece before crossing, out of sight of the sod house, and then circle round to come in well clear of the corral, to avoid disturbing the horses. But try as he might, Torn saw neither hide nor hair of the hunter until Longshot suddenly appeared on the roof. The lookout didn't know he was there until it was too late. Longshot Indianed up behind the unsuspecting man, clapped one hand over his mouth, and laid the blade of a hunting knife to his throat. The guard wisely chose discretion over valor. He didn't put up a fight. Longshot struck him behind the ear, a measured blow, using the iron ball of the knife's pommel, and the lookout sagged, out cold. The hunter caught the carbine as it slipped out of the guard's arms, and laid the unconscious man down gently.

Then he straightened up and looked across the river at the willow thicket where he had left Torn, and made a come-hither gesture.

Mounting the Palouse, Torn left the willows and crossed the shallow river, leading Longshot's horse. The water was running fast, tumbling over slick rocks, and he let the Appaloosa pick its way, keeping his attention focused on the soddy.

If any of the men inside glanced out a window or stepped through the door, they would not fail to see him. And if that happened, he could only hope their reaction would not be immediately hostile. They did not know him, and could not know his purpose, or that he had tracked them from the iron road, and consequently might wonder what his presence signified. If they came out to greet him with hot lead, he was in trouble. Out in the open like this, he was a goner.

As he made the crossing Longshot left the roof the way he had come, slipping around to the front with the guard's carbine—Torn noted it was an old Spencer 56/50. The hunter ducked under the window and took a position with his back to the wall to one side of the front door.

The door, stout timbers on rawhide hinges, was closed. So were the shutters on the two front windows. The shutters had crosshatched gun slots. Torn guessed this had once been an isolated homestead. He wondered what had happened to its original inhabitants. This was harsh country, barely suitable for raising livestock, and scarcely appropriate for farming. Perhaps the land had beaten the homesteaders, or maybe Indians had killed them or driven them away. Paiutes and Kiowas were still making nuisances of themselves in these parts.

Or maybe the men Torn was stalking had moved them out.

Torn got across the river without mishap. He dismounted in front of the soddy, bold as brass. Up close, he identified the cannon as a Whitworth. The Confederacy had imported some from England during the war. Excellent ordnance.

Drawing the Winchester 44/40 from its saddle ties, Torn walked up to the door. Longshot nodded, and Torn went right on in like he owned the place.

There were five men inside.

One sat at a rough-hewn table in the center of the room. He was playing a desultory game of solitaire with a dog-eared pack of pasteboards. The other four lay in their bunks, of which there were six, three sets of upper and lower, ranged around the walls. Three of the four men in the bunks seemed to be asleep, while the fourth was thumbing through a dime novel.

The man at the table had his back to the door. As Torn entered he turned. He wore faded long johns tucked into butternut-gray trousers. A forage cap bearing the letters *CSA* over crossed sabers was set at a jaunty angle on his head. When he saw Torn, his eyes got big and he reached for a pistol in his belt.

Torn didn't break stride. He slammed the stock of the Winchester against the man's skull. The man toppled sideways, jarring the table, hitting the hard-packed floor with a thump. Torn moved past the table, stepping over the man, as the fellow with the dime novel threw his wildcat literature aside and rolled out to lunge for a carbine leaning against a nearby wall. Torn leveled the Winchester.

"Don't," he said.

The man moved with surprising quickness.

He grabbed the Winchester's barrel and wrenched it downward. At the same time he threw a punch at Torn's face. The rock-hard fist connected, and the blow hurled Torn back into the table. Still grasping the barrel of the rifle, the man moved in. Torn let go of the Winchester, drove a fist into the man's belly and a forearm into his face. The man staggered. Torn bulled into him. The man tried to club him with the Winchester, but Torn ducked under and drove him back into a wall. The man dropped the rifle. A fist grazed Torn's chin. Another glanced off his shoulder. The man was grinning now. It was a bloody grin. He was a tough, scrappy fighter, and Torn respected him for that, giving no thought to resorting to the Colt Peacemaker or his saber-knife. He answered instead with three gut punches in quick succession and followed these up with a left hook. The man wheezed, grunted, and fell to his knees. Torn's boot caught him under the chin, and he was out for the count.

Breathing hard, Torn rubbed his knuckles and threw a quick look around the soddy.

Longshot was standing just inside the door. He had the other three men covered. Everybody had been watching the fight.

"I swear," drawled one of the men under Longshot's gun. "Never thought I'd see the day somebody'd come along and whup the cap'n."

The speaker was still on his bunk, propped up on an elbow. He looked mighty unconcerned.

"Get down out of there, soldier," snapped Torn.

The man complied, to stand with the other two.

All three wore at least one Confederate-issue garment.

"Who the hell are you men?" asked Torn.

They exchanged glances. No one responded.

"What unit is this?" Torn asked.

One of the men drew himself up into something resembling attention. "We're all that's left of Drayton's Horse Artillery, suh."

"Who's in command?"

"That'd be Cap'n Buck Drayton, suh." The speaker pointed at the man sprawled unconscious at Torn's feet. "As you can see, he's indisposed at the moment."

CHAPTER 6

TORN DREW THE PEACEMAKER.

"Boys, I want you to gather up all your weapons and pile them on the floor over there in front of the fireplace. Move slow, like molasses in winter. We've come this far without any killing, and I'd like to keep it that way."

The three did as they were told. Carbines, pistols, and knives were laid down near the hearth. No one made a wrong move. When they were done, Torn had them sit at the table. A bucket of river water was available, and he roused the unconscious Buck Drayton by dousing him with its contents.

Sputtering, Drayton sat up. He wiped water off his face, ruefully massaged his chin, and blinked up at Torn with more curiosity than animosity.

"You pack a hell of a punch," he said.

"That makes two of us, then."

"We'll have to go again someday."

"That's fine with me."

Drayton grinned and spat blood. He crossed on hands and knees to the man Torn had knocked out with the butt of the Winchester. Like all good officers, Drayton's foremost concern was the welfare of his troops. He felt for the man's pulse and checked his gashed scalp.

"How's ol' Bushrod, Cap'n?" asked one of the men at the table.

"He'll be all right," replied Drayton. "He's got a hard head."

He rose and faced Torn. "I suppose we are your prisoners, sir," he said with stiff formality.

"I suppose so, Captain."

"What of Corporal Tuttle? He was the man I posted as lookout."

"He's sleepin'," said Longshot.

"For how long?"

"Not forever."

Drayton looked relieved.

"We tracked seven of you," said Torn. "Someone's missing."

"He's not here," said Drayton.

"One of your command?"

"Yes."

"What's his name and where did he go?"

"Don't waste your time," said Drayton. "As soldiers, we are required to give you no more information than our names and rank."

"Captain, you are soldiers in an army that no longer exists."

Drayton frowned. He was as tall as Torn, and heftier; his unruly hair was blond, but the stubble of beard on his cheeks was brown. His features were square, tenacious looking. His blue eyes were quick and piercing.

"We never surrendered. We went into Mexico with General Shelby. There were twenty of us then. We had three guns. One was a Napoleon. But we're down to what you see before us. There has been quite a bit of action down in Mexico these past years."

"I know. So you've turned into mercenaries, then."

"We're Confederate soldiers, sir."

"Fighting for whichever side pays the best?"

"You're looking for another fight, I take it."

"Smooth your hackles, Captain."

"We know no other life," said Drayton, defensive. "I was not yet twenty when the War for Southern Independence was declared, and all these boys were even younger. We all hail from Crockett County, Tennessee. We grew up together and now we fight together."

Torn looked them over, aware that he was in the presence of true warriors—men who had lived by the sword for almost eighteen years. The experiences that had forged them into a fighting unit had forged them into a brotherhood as well. They were trail-hardened and battle-tested, seasoned veterans in every sense of the word.

This was manifest in the way they conducted themselves now. They weren't going to make any foolish moves. They would wait, calmly, confident in themselves, and look for an opening. Above all, they would act honorably, the way soldiers should. They weren't concerned about their predicament—no doubt they had been in worse.

"How did you get tied in with the Coastal and Northern?" Torn asked Drayton.

"We used to serve with Colonel Stinson in the Army of the Tennessee. He contacted us in Mexico. Said he was competing with a railroad run by Yankees."

"And I bet that's all he had to say to get you boys to come running," said Torn dryly.

"General Rhynes is running the show for the Great Western, and what Southerner doesn't remember him? He hasn't been playing fair. Colonel Stinson has taken all of his underhanded ways that he intends to take. He will fight fire with fire."

"You've got it backward. Stinson's the one who's not playing by the rules."

"I would expect you to say so, since clearly you are in the employ of the Great Western."

"No," said Torn. "I'm a federal judge. But before that I was a colonel in the Confederate army. The First South Carolina Cavalry, formerly part of Hampton's Brigade."

Drayton was startled by this revelation. "Your name, sir?"

"Clayton Randall Torn."

"You're a federal judge?"

"That's right. You see, the war is over."

"Not for everybody," said one of the rebel artillerymen.

"That'll be enough, Private Rosser," snapped Drayton. "Well then, Judge, what do you intend to do with us?"

"What do you think I should do? Yesterday you fired on unarmed civilians."

"Nonsense. I venture to say not a single person was injured. We fired two warning shots before we destroyed that engine."

"You were getting your range."

"No, sir. We had our range. My God, man, we were sitting up there on that ridge waiting for the train. We had the range marked before nightfall."

"Still, you might have missed your mark. People could have been killed."

"We have never been responsible for the death of a noncombatant," Drayton insisted.

"Besides," drawled Private Rosser, "we don't never miss."

Torn mulled it over. He was inclined to believe these men. They were soldiers, and soldiers did not wage war on civilians—not true soldiers, anyway. But they were misguided, on the wrong side of this railroad feud.

"What are we gonna do with 'em, Judge?" asked Longshot.

Torn shook his head. These men had fought for the Confederacy, as he had, and even now, after all these years, he felt an old and musty but abiding fraternity.

"Okay," he said at length. "You seem to think you are fighting a war here. In that case, you are prisoners of war."

"I guess we'll have to go along with that," said Drayton.

"Then I will offer all of you parole, on the condition that you will not again raise a hand against the Great Western. If Stinson is the soldier you think he is, he'll have no choice but to abide by that condition, if you accept it."

Drayton rubbed his chin, glancing at the other three diehard Rebels.

"And the alternative?"

"I'll haul the lot of you into Alamosa, lock you in a

jail cell, and put you on trial as common criminals when I have the time."

"Trial? In Alamosa? That's a Great Western town. What chance would we have with Great Western men on the jury?"

Torn shrugged. "The fact that almost everybody in Alamosa either works for or makes his living on account of the Great Western can't be helped."

"We'd hang for sure," said Drayton. "Or at the very least spend the next twenty years in prison."

"Then I suggest you take me up on my offer. It would be the soldier's way."

Drayton sighed. "I guess you're being more than fair. Are we allowed to keep our sidearms?"

"Yes."

"And the Whitworth?"

"Spike it."

Drayton stiffened. "We can't do that."

"It can do nothing but get you into trouble."

"She's all we have. I guess it's Alamosa."

Torn grimaced. "Very well. I'll let you keep the damned thing."

"You'll accept my word of honor?"

"I will."

Drayton proffered a hand. "Then you have it."

"You'll wage no more war on the Great Western?"

"We won't," Drayton promised. "None of us."

Torn shook his hand.

"YOU REALLY TRUST THEM BOYS?" LONGSHOT QUERIED
as he and Torn rode back across the river.

By his tone of voice it was clear that the hunter did
not. He kept looking over his shoulder, as though he
expected Drayton and his men to come busting out
of the soddy with guns blazing.

"Call it a calculated risk," replied Torn.

He did not once look back.

"I'm just wondering what General Rhynes and
Orly Bracken will call it?"

"Doesn't matter. I don't answer to Bracken or the
general. Or anybody else."

"Well, I still got an itch between the shoulder
blades," Longshot confessed. "Don't know much
about this soldier's code of honor and such. Where I
come from it's mostly Injuns you trade lead with, and
an Injun will give you all kinds of sweet talk to your

face—and then stick a knife in your back soon as
you turn around."

"We're not dealing with Indians."

"Nope, we ain't," allowed the hunter.

They rode on a ways in silence.

"I hope you're right about them," Longshot said
eventually. "That's a heck of a big gun them boys is
draggin' all around the countryside. Sure could do
some damage."

Torn nodded. He could remember all too well the
kind of damage a twelve-pounder could do.

They headed north and a little west. Longshot
took the lead. He declared he was able to lead them
straight into Whiskey Flat, and Torn relied on him to
do so.

He was as good as his word.

It took them all day to get there, and late that
afternoon a storm came roaring down out of the
mountains—what Torn hoped would prove to be the
last of the winter's storms. Fortunately Longshot
had an extra slicker, so Torn wasn't completely
soaked by the rain and sleet when they rode into the
end-of-track boomtown.

By this time the storm front had moved on south.
The rain had turned the wide streets of Whiskey Flat
into treacherous quagmires of yellow clay. The sun
had set behind the mountains. The first stars flick-
ered in a greenish sky between shreds of purple-
black clouds. Despite the conditions of the streets
and a bitter, biting wind, the boomtown was ablaze
with lights and bustling with activity.

Men were cursing and straining to free a mired
freight wagon. Others were securing the guy ropes
of a brand-new tent saloon. They, too, were cursing
as the capricious wind made their work harder than

it should have been. Somewhere off on the dark edge of town someone was shooting a gun. Torn hoped the target was the sky. But he did not hope too much. He was well acquainted with such places as Whiskey Flat. Life was quick and cheap and death could come without warning.

Last year Whiskey Flat had been a barren stretch of alkali and sagebrush. Its only residents had been the sidewinder and the coyote and the Gila monster. Next year could be likewise. But this year a town had sprung into existence, raw and new and altogether unattractive. Lumber had been hauled down off the mountain flanks and raw-board shanties and tent cabins had been thrown up in reckless haste. The purpose was to provide shelter, not to be pleasing to the eye. Nobody gave a hoot how they looked. The streets, four of them and all running north-south, were wide enough to turn a wagon in, and anybody who wanted to could put up a structure along one of them.

Most of the businesses were designed with one purpose in mind—to separate the railroad workers from their hard-earned pay. This applied to the dozens of saloons and bordellos, of course, but defined as well every barbershop, bath house, mercantile, and eatery.

By far the biggest and most eye-catching enterprise was a place called the Shamrock. If the sign, with its emerald-green four-leaf clovers, wasn't sufficient to draw one's attention, the big blue-and-white circus tent that served as the establishment's roof would surely do the trick. As he rode by, Torn listened to the barkers at the door rolling out their spiel to hook passersby.

"Come on in, sports! Try your luck with the prettiest ladies west of Wichita! Give us a bet at an honest table. Poker. Blackjack. Faro. We got it all. Step right in, buckos, and sample the finest whiskey in Whiskey Flat!"

From within came the strains of a gallopade, played by a competent brass band—and played loudly so as to be heard over the rumble of a hundred voices and the thunder of bootheels on the dance floor. Men were pouring in and out of the place, and Torn thought of all the money going from the Great Western's coffers, with only a brief interim residence in the pockets of the paddies who worked the iron road, into the hands of the man who owned the Shamrock.

"Who runs that place?" he asked Longshot.

"Feller named Gellhorn. An Englishman. He speaks for all the men who run these shanty hells. In spite of his pedigree, the Irish boys flock to his bar. Like the barker says, he's got the best whiskey and the prettiest women in town."

"Honest tables?"

Longshot's grin was sly. "I didn't go that far."

They were past the Shamrock when a commotion from behind compelled them to turn their horses sharply.

A man came through the Shamrock's doorway and landed on his back in the mustard-colored muck of the street. He got up, bellowing in a drunken rage, and charged forward, intent on reentry. A man with *bouncer* written all over him suddenly appeared in the doorway to block his path. The bouncer wielded a hickory club about two feet long, with rawhide wrapped tightly around one end to serve as a grip. As the other man bulled forward, growling like a wounded grizzly, the bouncer clubbed him viciously.

The man went down, blood a scarlet mask on his face. The bouncer kicked him, rolling him back into the mud.

Several more men came boiling out of the Shamrock—Irish railroaders by the look of them. While two of them launched a verbal attack on the bouncer, the third went to his injured comrade and rolled him over onto his back. That was a smart thing to do, mused Torn, as a man could drown in this viscous mess.

Instinctively drawn to trouble, and sensing that more violence was imminent, Torn urged the Appaloosa forward.

The bouncer menaced the two who besieged him with the hickory club. The pair shook their gnarly fists at him. No one but Torn paid any attention to the man who had knelt beside the bouncer's grievously injured victim. This one was surreptitiously drawing a pistol from under his coat as he stood. He did not notice Torn behind him, so intent was he on the altercation taking place in front of the Shamrock. So he was caught by surprise when Torn planted a boot between his shoulder blades.

The man sprawled face-first in the mud. He turned over and sat up and looked into the barrel of the Colt Peacemaker in Torn's hand.

He looked at the gun as though at first he did not realize what it was. Then he groped around in the muck for the pistol he had drawn from beneath his coat and subsequently lost in his fall.

Torn thumbed the Colt's hammer back.

The loud and lethal double click seemed to bring the man to his senses. His whole body went rigid and he stopped feeling around in the yellow mud for his gun, which had sunk out of sight.

The bouncer and the two Irishmen near the Shamrock's door turned their attention to Torn, and now one of the Irishmen stepped forward, slogging through the mire, to position himself between Torn and the man at whom Torn was pointing the Peacemaker. His stance and demeanor were defiant and belligerent. The Colt did not seem to scare him.

"And just what do you think you're doin'?" he asked, his brogue heavy and his tone reproachful.

"Just keeping the peace," was Torn's unruffled reply. "That's my job."

"Keepin' the peace," echoed the other, caustic. "With a forty-five-caliber Colt revolver."

"You'd be surprised how well it works."

"JUST WHO ARE YOU?"

"Clay Torn. Federal judge. And you?"

"Macauley Rourke. Friends call me Collie. I'm president of the Irish Brigade."

"What's an Irish Brigade?"

"A labor organization. A union, established to look out for the health and well-bein' of the naddies who work the iron road. Officially we're the Railroaders' Benevolent Association. Irish Brigade, for short."

"Any relation to the Molly Maguires?"

Collie Rourke scowled.

The Molly Maguires had been a labor organization founded in the Pennsylvania coalfields for the purpose of improving the lot of Irish miners. The miners had been exploited in every conceivable way; their working conditions had been hazardous, to say the least, their company-provided housing deplorable, their wages an outrage. The mine owners, mostly of English and Welsh descent, treated them with contempt, and they could get no help from the government, either state or federal, which at the time had been under the influence of isolationist Know-Nothings, who considered Irish immigrants second-class citizens.

After peaceful means had failed them, the Molly Maguires had lost their patience and resorted to violence. The union had always had a militant bent—it had to have in order to survive, much less prevail, against the brutal practices of management. Mine bosses were beaten, some murdered. Company property was destroyed or seized. Riots erupted from one end of the Pennsylvania coal country to the other, and matters got so desperately bad that the state militia had to be called in to maintain order.

Torn did not want to see a similar situation arise here on the railroad.

"What would you be tryin' to say?" challenged Collie Rourke.

"That depends on what you boys are trying to do."

A crowd was gathering. Men heading into the Shamrock were pausing to watch the confrontation, and several more had emerged from the saloon to see what the ruckus was all about.

Torn noticed out of the corner of his eye that Longshot had his Sharps buffalo gun slanted across his saddle. The rifle was still sheathed in that beaded and fringed buckskin cover, but the hunter had his finger on the trigger, and he was watching the crowd and Torn's back. That made Torn feel a lot better about the situation, because it looked like most of the crowd were Irish railroad workers, and they looked sympathetic to Collie Rourke.

"We just want to make sure our people get a fair shake," said Collie.

"You have some complaints about the way the Great Western's been treating you?"

"A few. But none that canna be worked out with Rhynes and Bracken and that crowd. Orly Bracken's a tightfisted, ornery cuss, but he's fair-minded. Our real problems lie with the two-legged snakes who operate these bloody dives." Collie glowered at the bouncer, who was standing his ground in front of the Shamrock's door.

"I daresay he is referring to me, for one."

This came from a man who had just emerged from the Shamrock and then stepped to one side to distance himself from the bouncer. He was a tall, slender man, neatly clad in a blue clawhammer coat, gold satin vest, nankeen trousers, and polished half boots. His hair was cotton white and longish. It was hard to determine his age—he looked very trim and fit and moved with a powerful grace.

For the first time Collie noticed this man standing off to one side, and by Rourke's expression Torn could tell there was no love lost between the two.

"Aye!" exclaimed Collie. "There's the worst of the lot. English Jack himself."

"John Gellhorn," said the white-haired man, addressing Torn. "These Irish buffoons can't even perform a simple introduction." There was mockery in his tone.

"Buffoons!" cried an irate Collie. "Why, you limey bastard . . ."

Gellhorn's derisive chuckle was a dry, rasping thing. "How articulate." He returned to Torn. "And who, may I ask, are you, sir?"

Torn told him.

"Ah yes," said Gellhorn, his voice silky smooth. "I've heard you were coming. On the train that was waylaid today, I believe."

"Waylaid? Blown to hell and gone would be more accurate."

Gellhorn tsk-tsked. "A dastardly business. Did you catch the miscreants responsible?"

"They've been taken care of."

"Splendid. Then allow me to offer you a drink, on the house. A small gesture, out of gratitude for a job well done."

"Maybe later," said Torn, aware that Collie was watching him suspiciously. It would not do to be seen taking sides.

Gellhorn shrugged. "And what happened here?" He made a sweeping gesture, which included the bouncer, Collie, and the unconscious man in the mud of the street.

"Your assassin tried to break Will Flaherty's head open," said Collie.

Gellhorn arched an eyebrow. "He is not an assassin. He is employed to keep the peace in my establishment. You Irish boys can get unruly at times, and you often must be persuaded to pay what you owe." He turned to the bouncer. "What happened?"

"It's just like you said, Mr. Gellhorn. He ordered a bottle of whiskey and drunk it up before anybody could say otherwise, and then he said he couldn't pay. So I tossed him out. Then he came at me. I was just defendin' myself."

"There, you see?" Gellhorn addressed this to Torn.

"Will's poke was stolen while he was in your place," said Collie. "He didn't know it till he went to pay for his bottle."

"I admit that there is, unfortunately, riffraff among my clientele."

Collie clenched his fists. "If there's riffraff in the Shamrock, you hired it. Everybody knows you keep pickpockets working the crowd."

"Slanderous lies," Gellhorn declared, with casual indifference.

"That's enough," Torn said sharply.

Everybody looked at him.

"Mr. Gellhorn, from now on, if you have a problem in your place, you send for me. I'll take care of it. That's what I'm here for. To take care of problems. And as for you, Mr. Rourke, and your Irish Brigade, you bring your complaints to me and I'll look into it. Don't make the mistake of taking the law into your own hands."

"Who's side are you on?" asked Collie, clearly skeptical.

"I'm on the side of law and order. Now, get your friend to a doctor. While you stand there arguing, he's lying there bleeding to death."

"Yes, please do," said Gellhorn, looking at the injured man with disdain. "Blood is bad for business."

With that he turned on his heel and went back inside the Shamrock.

C H A P T E R

9

ENGLISH JACK GELLHORN PROCEEDED IMMEDIATELY TO his office in the rear of the Shamrock.

His saloon had been moved a half-dozen times in the past eighteen months, but this transient state of affairs did not prevent Gellhorn from running a first-class operation. The cornerstone of his enterprise was the impressive seventy-five-foot portable bar. This unique invention could be separated into two parts; the two halves were fashioned in such a way that when it was closed down and all the contents secured, axles could be attached to underpinnings and the whole show transported from one spot to another over fairly rough country with a minimum of breakage.

The gaming tables and chairs were hauled by wagon, as was the canvas tent roof. Gellhorn employed a small army of men who had become very skilled at moving the Shamrock. It was no happy accident that most of them were skilled as well in breaking bones and busting heads.

As in previous incarnations, the Whiskey Flat version of the Shamrock was as sturdy and weatherproof as any structure in the boomtown. The walls were made with logs of mountain pine hauled down out of the high country and carefully chinked. The saloon even sported a solid wood floor—which was something less than half of Whiskey Flat's other establishments could at present boast of.

Floor and walls were put in place first, and the canvas tent strapped down securely, held aloft by stout poles. The interior was one big room, with the exception of Gellhorn's inner sanctum. The backdoor led to a row of tents where the women of easy virtue English Jack employed on a percentage basis plied the world's oldest profession.

Gellhorn's office—also his sleeping quarters—was evidence of the English adventurer's conviction that a gentleman did not have to forsake the comfort that was his due just because he happened to find himself on the American frontier.

The furnishings included a walnut desk, an impressive oak sideboard, a plush velveteen settee, and behind a folding wooden screen, a camp bed. Set in a back corner of the saloon, the office had two additional walls that separated it from the rest of the place. These interior walls were seven feet high, also of chinked pine logs. Two pieces of canvas extended from the top of the interior walls to the tent roof, and were sewn onto the latter, providing Gellhorn with complete privacy. The office had two doors, one to the saloon proper, the other leading outside.

It was through the latter that Gellhorn's visitor

had come just prior to the altercation between the Shamrock bouncer and the Irish Brigade, and English Jack found him waiting patiently when he returned to the office. Gellhorn was particularly glad for the privacy the office afforded him, because this visitor was one it would not do to publicly associate with.

While waiting for Gellhorn to come back, the visitor had helped himself to the selection of liquor displayed in glass decanters atop the sideboard. He had also removed the greatcoat he had been wearing upon arrival, and now Gellhorn had an opportunity to examine with curiosity his guest's butternut-gray military tunic. The tunic, with its red collar and cuffs and piping, was quite a bit frayed and faded, English Jack noted. It appeared to be a garment that had survived much hard campaigning. As did the man who wore it.

"Sergeant Gregg, accept my apologies for the delay."

Sergeant Gregg shrugged and knocked back the shot of whiskey. It wasn't his first. He gasped as the liquor exploded inside him. His smile was positively beatific.

"Damn good," he drawled, and belched.

"The best money can buy," Gellhorn replied, circling the desk to take his chair. "Help yourself."

Gregg was already back at the sideboard. "Thanks. Don't mind if I do."

He poured himself another shot and meandered over to stand across the desk from English Jack. He gazed with idle curiosity at Gellhorn.

"You talk funny. You British?"

"Quite. And, like yourself, a military man. Retired,

of course. First Leftenant, Twenty-first Royal Fusiliers. Saw action in the Crimea."

Gregg kept staring. Gellhorn's martial credentials did not seem to impress him all that much. He just grunted.

"How come you British never did he'p us Confederates?" he asked. "You all talked a mighty good game, but nothin' come of it."

Gellhorn's smile was faintly deprecating. "It's rather complicated, and I wouldn't want to bore you, Sergeant."

Gregg missed the unflattering implications of that remark. "Well," he drawled, "it's too damn late now, ain't it? What matters now is the money Colonel Stinson promised us."

"I am familiar with the arrangement he made with your captain . . . Drayton, isn't it? Two hundred American dollars for every Great Western locomotive destroyed."

Gregg nodded enthusiastically. "We kilt one of them iron horses yesterday. Cap'n sent me to collect. You're the paymaster."

"That I am." Gellhorn removed a metal cash box from a desk drawer, opened it, and extracted a thin stack of greenbacks. These he placed on top of the desk in front of Gregg. "Feel free to count it."

"Nothin' personal," said Gregg, and did so. "All here."

"Then, if you are satisfied, I suggest you return to your compatriots with all due haste and make certain that they are well."

"Huh?"

Gellhorn replaced the cash box in the desk drawer and rose to go to the sideboard and pour himself a glass of Napoleon brandy. "There is a man in town," he told the Confederate. "A Judge Torn. Apparently he was on that train you and your friends wrecked. I am told he and another man, a hunter named Gant, pursued your unit after the locomotive was destroyed."

Gregg cocked his head to one side and squinted at Gellhorn. "Mebbe so. But they didn't catch us."

"It is possible that they did so after your captain sent you here."

"The boys can take care of themselves."

"Torn and Gant arrived here in Whiskey Flat tonight."

"Then they must've give up trackin' us."

"Torn doesn't strike me as the kind who would give up."

"Must've," Gregg insisted obstinately. "Iffen he caught up with the cap'n and the rest of the outfit, he and this Gant feller would be laid out stone-cold dead."

"Perhaps. But Torn told me he'd taken care of the men who had waylaid the train. Perhaps he was lying. At any rate, it was merely a suggestion." He raised his glass. "Here's to the Coastal and Northern."

"And to more dead Great Western engines," Gregg added with a yellow grin. "Worth two hundred Yankee greenbacks a pop."

There came a knock on the door to the saloon.

"Mr. Gellhorn?"

Gregg's hand dropped to the pistol in his belt. He knew he was in the enemy camp.

"Relax," Gellhorn said under his breath. "It's one of my men. You had best be on your way, Sergeant. Wouldn't do for anyone to see us together. No one in Whiskey Flat knows I work with Stinson and the

Coastal and Northern, and I prefer to keep it that way. These Irishmen would like any excuse to treat me to a necktie party."

Gregg gathered up his greatcoat, pocketed the two hundred dollars, and slipped out the other door into the deepening night without a backward glance.

"Mr. Gellhorn? You in there?"

"Come in, Logan."

The man entered. He wore a bartender's apron and a harried expression on his face.

"There's a woman out here wants to see you."

"A woman?"

"Says she needs work."

"Ah." Gellhorn smiled. "That kind of woman."

Logan shrugged, ambivalent.

"Send her in, then."

Logan stepped out and spoke to someone Gellhorn could not see—someone who was waiting just beyond the door.

"He'll see you, miss."

When the woman crossed the threshold, English Jack Gellhorn knew at a glance she was special. Not at all like most of the women who worked for him. This one was by far the prettiest woman in Whiskey Flat—if not in the entire American West. Gellhorn was instantly captivated by her pale, delicate beauty, and bewitched by her alluring smoke-gray eyes. He stepped up, took her hand, raised it to his lips, and performed a crisp continental bow.

"John Gellhorn, ma'am, at your service," he said gallantly.

"Rachel Bailey," she said. "We have never met, but I have heard of you, Mr. Gellhorn. I was told . . . I was told you are a gentleman." She lowered her gaze demurely.

By someone who doesn't know me very well, thought English Jack. But he replied, "I like to think so."

"I am in . . . rather desperate straits."

"My dear, you have come to the right place. Damsels in distress are my specialty." He bestowed his most charming smile upon her.

"Do you think you might see fit to help me?"

"I'm sure something can be arranged," said English Jack.

CHAPTER 10

"I MET MARTIN KELSO IN BALTIMORE," SAID RACHEL. "I was born there. Martin was attending the academy at West Point. He was in his fourth year when we met. We fell in love. He asked me to marry him. I said yes. He promised we would marry as soon as he graduated. If I am boring you . . ."

"Certainly not," said Gellhorn. "Please continue, Miss Bailey."

Rachel took a quick look around. She sat with Gellhorn at a table in the rear of the Shamrock. The saloon was going great guns, with much noise and action. Men were lined up at the bar three deep. Every table was packed. Not a vacant chair to be found. The brass band was up on their platform, playing with vigor. Women were working the crowd, trying to get the men to buy them drinks and dance with them. The drinks were a prerequisite for the next step: the tents out back. Rachel paid the percentage girls special interest. Gellhorn thought she had a haunted look in her eyes.

"My family did not approve of Martin," she continued, with a soulful sigh. "My father owns a shipping business. He thought I could do much better for myself. I think he still believes in those old-fashioned arrangements, where love has nothing to do with marriage. After all, Martin would graduate the academy with the rank of lieutenant, and in all likelihood be sent to the frontier to fight Indians, and there simply isn't much chance for promotion in the army these days, and a lieutenant's pay is—" She stopped and took a deep breath. "I apologize for rambling on."

"Don't mention it."

"I realized my father only wanted the best for me. He did not care to see his only daughter exposed to the hardships and heartache of life in a frontier army post. But I refused to listen. I was madly in love with Martin. I would have followed him to the ends of the earth, if necessary.

"As we anticipated, Martin was assigned to a remote post in Nebraska immediately upon his graduation from West Point. He had to report with such haste that there was no chance of getting married in Baltimore, and besides, my father had still not consented. Martin urged me to elope. But I just couldn't do that. It would have shamed my family, you understand."

"I understand perfectly."

"I promised to follow him to Nebraska as soon as I could. When my father discovered my plans, he tried to prevent me from going. We had a terrible row. He warned me that if I insisted on this foolish course, I would not be welcome in his house again. Once I left, I could never return. Of course that did not deter me."

"Of course not," Gellhorn said gently. " 'Love knows nothing of order,' according to St. Jerome."

"So I left Baltimore and arrived in Nebraska only to find that Martin had . . . had . . ." Tears welled up in her eyes.

"There, there," Gellhorn soothed, brandishing a monogrammed handkerchief. "My poor child."

Rachel composed herself. "He had taken up with an Indian woman. I am afraid I made a terrible scene."

"You had every right to do so."

"Martin was furious. I was making a fool of him, and of myself, in front of the garrison. I . . . I simply wanted to die. All my dreams came crashing down. I was heartbroken."

"The scoundrel ought to be shot," Gellhorn declared with righteous indignation. "He must have been blind as well."

"You are very kind, Mr. Gellhorn."

"I hope in time you see fit to call me Jack. All my friends do."

"After the confrontation with Martin, I was at a loss as to what to do with myself. What could I do? I couldn't go back home to Baltimore. I was too ashamed. And, I suppose, perhaps, too proud to go crawling back to Father. Would my circle of friends accept me back into the fold? I thought it unlikely. Having chased Martin all the way to Nebraska, I was in essence a fallen woman."

Brimming with sympathy, Gellhorn nodded.

"I understand the situation very well," he said. "You see, I was the black sheep of my family. I resorted to service in the military to make my way. The doors to what is called high society were firmly closed to me."

"I had very little money," said Rachel. "The journey west had taken almost every bit I had. I went to work in a restaurant in Omaha, only to find that the owner expected more from me than an honest day's work. He . . . tried to force his intentions upon me one night. When I resisted, he threw me out into the street."

Gellhorn shook his head and sighed. "Not all men are like that one, or your young lieutenant, Miss Bailey. I hope you know that."

"I was rescued by a woman who . . . well, she was . . ." Rachel blushed. "I must admit, at that point I was even considering her kind of work, just to stay alive. Fortunately this woman—her name was Rosalee—told me I should come to you. She said you would help me. She seemed to know you, and think quite highly of you, in her way."

Gellhorn raised an eyebrow. He racked his brain, yet could not exhume any recollection of a woman named Rosalee. No doubt, though, there had been such a woman in his past. There had been many women. So many, in fact, that he thought he deserved to be excused for failing to recall every name.

His appetite for women was notorious. His debonair style drew them as a flame attracted moths. He used them and discarded them and he never looked back. For one thing, he did not believe in love. At least not the kind of which the poets spoke. He did not think there was a woman alive who could hold him like that. He thought women were fickle creatures. His mother certainly had been. Her leaving had wrecked his father. His father had been living proof that love was the great destroyer, and it was a lesson Gellhorn never forgot.

Some of the women he left by the wayside had been bitter—had known they were being used and then thrown away. They had tried to escape their fate by claiming to love him. But English Jack had known better. It was all a question of power, and they simply could not stomach the fact that he maintained the upper hand, that he was the one to say when the relationship ended. He was determined always to be the one to leave, rather than, like his father, the one left.

And then there were a few women—poor, silly girls—who clung to their affection for him even after he had dumped them. There were fewer of the latter than the former, but he supposed this Rosalee was one.

"I assure you, Miss Bailey," he said, "you have no need to fear. You will be provided for."

She lowered her eyes, hands clasped tightly in her lap. "And . . . and what must I do?"

"Absolutely nothing. It is my duty as a gentleman to assist you. A duty, I might add, which I perform with pleasure."

"But I feel I must do something."

"Well, bartending and dancing with the customers is out of the question." Gellhorn pursed his lips. "Do you have an acquaintance with cards?"

"A little."

"Not poker, I daresay."

"I'm afraid not."

"Then, if you are willing, I will teach you, and you may then have your own table here. But under no circumstances will you be subjected to any rough attention by my clientele."

"Well, yes, I suppose I could do that."

"It isn't necessary, you understand. I could provide you with sufficient funds to take you anywhere you wish to go."

"Oh, no. I will stay and work for it."

"Then we have a deal."

"You are too kind, Mr. Gellhorn. I don't know how I will ever repay you."

Gellhorn made a dismissive gesture, as though it was of no consequence. But he knew exactly how she would repay him.

First, though, there was the game to be played.

CHAPTER 11

AFTER COLLIE ROURKE AND HIS IRISH BRIGADE associates had carried the wounded man away and the crowd, sensing that there would be no more bloody entertainment, had dispersed, Torn and Longshot left the Shamrock and continued on up the street.

The railroad cut across the north end of town, and even now, in this muddy, windy night, men were hard at work there. A construction train was heading west, where, a few miles out into the sagebrush, the tracks ended. On a siding stood a boarding train, which could house a thousand workers. As had been the case in Alamosa, stacks of iron rails and cross ties, as well as crates and barrels of other stores, loomed high in the gusty darkness.

Torn asked a crew foreman where he might find Orly Bracken, and was directed to a Pullman car sitting on a siding a stone's throw from the boarding train. As he and Longshot rode up, a man who looked too brawny and rough-hewn for the broadcloth suit he wore emerged onto the Pullman's vestibule and fired up a long nine. His face was craggy. His fleshy nose had been broken more than once. His beard was close cut and the color of rust.

Puffing on his cigar, the man grinned as he recognized Longshot.

"Gant! By God, you made it through another winter in those damned mountains. Come down out of the high lonesome to do some more hunting for the Great Western, I take it."

"Well," drawled Longshot, "I'll be doing some hunting, true enough. But maybe not the kind you mean, Niles. This feller here is Judge Clay Torn. Judge, this is Niles Keach."

Keach pumped Torn's hand vigorously. "Got a telegram from the general about you, Judge. Heard you were on that train that got blown to smithereens. What in heaven's name happened? Some of the men were saying something about a cannon?"

Torn nodded. "It's a long story."

Keach took the hint. "Come on in. Orly will want to hear it, too, and you'll only want to tell it once."

Torn expected the interior of the car to be as elegant as other private Pullmans he had seen. He was in for a surprise. The car had been completely renovated, divided into two functional offices. In the first were three cluttered desks. A young man wearing an eyeshade and sleeve garters was poring over a map at one of them. He scarcely looked up from his work as the three men filed past.

Niles Keach led the way into the second office, that belonging to the Great Western's superintendent of construction. Orly Bracken proved to be a small, wiry individual, gray and bespectacled and slightly stooped. Torn thought he looked like a man who was not yet fully recovered from a debilitating illness. But Bracken's grip was surprisingly robust, and his eyes were as sharp as a hawk's. His voice was full of vim and vigor.

He seemed to be overjoyed to see Torn. "You're the man we need, Judge," he declared. "If anybody can pin the Coastal and Northern's ears back, it'll be you. Now, what's all this about a cannon?"

"It's true," said Torn, and told all that needed to be told about Captain Buck Drayton and his rebel field-piece. By the time he had finished, Bracken looked a lot less happy.

"You paroled them?" the superintendent asked irritably. "What makes you think you can trust such . . . such scoundrels?"

Longshot gave Torn an I-told-you-so look.

"They're soldiers," replied Torn. "Drayton gave his word of honor as an officer and a gentleman. He'll keep it."

Bracken scowled. "You were a Confederate officer yourself, weren't you?"

"I was," said Torn. "But that has nothing to do with this. About all Captain Drayton has left is his honor, and he won't sully it by going back on his word. I'm sure of it."

"A cannon," Keach mused. "By God, they could have done some damage with a damned cannon. Leave it to Ezra Stinson to come up with something like that."

"He'll have a few more surprises up his sleeve this year, I assure you," said Bracken sourly. "We're in for a long pull, gentlemen. As if Stinson and his antics aren't enough, we have the weather conspiring against us, too, it seems."

"If it's against us," said Keach, "it's against the Coastal and Northern, too. We've got further to go to reach Wolf Creek Pass, but in the beginning, at least, we have an easier go of it than they do."

"Then if he's smart," said Torn, "Stinson will throw everything he has against the Great Western right now."

"To top it all off," said Bracken, "we have rogues like John Gellhorn luring our men astray with their liquor and painted ladies."

"All work and no play is not and never will be an Irish motto," declared Keach. He turned to Torn. "I know these buckos. I should—I'm one of them. Don't let these duds fool you. Not too many years ago I laid iron for the UP, at two dollars a day. I know it's a damned nuisance, but those shanty hells are a necessary evil. The men have got to cut loose every now and then, or they won't work."

"But how many report unfit for work every morning?" Bracken complained. "If I had my way, I'd send Gellhorn and all the rest of those vice barons packing."

"Then you wouldn't have a man jack left on the payroll," said Keach. "We have to live with it, Orly. If you want them to lay rail, you'll have to let them raise hell, too."

"I'm inclined to agree," said Torn. "It's the Coastal and Northern that brought me here. I'll try to keep a lid on Whiskey Flat at the same time."

"That's a tall order," said Bracken. "You'll need twenty, thirty men to provide us with adequate protection, if you ask me."

"So far I've found one." Torn aimed a thumb in Longshot's direction.

"Last year Stinson's hired guns were taking potshots at our grading crews up ahead and blowing up sections of track behind us. As a result, we were only able to lay two hundred and forty miles of track. This year we've got to do better. The Coastal and Northern is fifty miles closer to Wolf Creek Pass. That's two days. They took Durango from us last year, and if they take the mining towns away this year, we'll lose our charter for sure and go belly-up. Nobody needs a railroad that doesn't go anywhere."

"We'll do what we can," said Torn coolly. Bracken struck him as a desperate man, and desperate men made him nervous. "Right now, though, I could use a shave and a meal and a bed to sleep in."

"We've got a Pullman for your personal use," said Bracken, "and a boxcar for your mounts. A Jupiter and its crew will be at your disposal twenty-four hours a day."

"I'll show you," said Keach.

"And be advised," said Bracken, "that on top of everything else, we've heard a rumor the Kiowas are on the warpath. Personally I wouldn't be at all surprised if Stinson's agents aren't the ones stirring them up."

CHAPTER

12

THE NEXT MORNING BEFORE DAWN TORN'S PRIVATE train headed west out of Whiskey Flat.

The train consisted of a Jupiter ten-wheeler, a tender, the Pullman, and a boxcar. The latter had been converted into a stables on wheels, with stalls and a stock of hay and oats. The Pullman had a combination office/parlor and an adjoining bedroom. Torn found the accommodations more than satisfactory, and had given Longshot the parlor as his quarters for the night.

"But don't get used to it," Torn had told the hunter. "You'll be spending most of your nights out on the plains."

"Suits me," said Longshot. "I just sleep better under the stars than under a roof."

They could not go far by rail that morning and left the train at end-of-track to proceed on horseback.

Past several supply trains they rode, where long lines of freight wagons waited, destined to transfer supplies from these trains to the grading camps and bridge crews strewn fifty miles and more ahead.

Though the sun had not yet risen, hundreds of men were hard at work, laboring by the light of towering construction fires that danced in the blustery wind. For a while Torn watched them work. An engine delivered a load of rails. The load was dumped and the rails manhandled onto horse-drawn trucks, which in turn moved the steel to end-of-track. The steel gang jumped in then; four men to a rail, and two rails were run forward and laid down on the cross ties already in place. A gauger checked them and jumped out of the way as the spikers advanced to nail the rails down with their spikes and sledge-hammers. The bolters were next, in and out quickly, and one more section was made. The horse-drawn trucks moved forward again, and the steel gang performed the same service for the next section, followed by gauger, spikers, and bolters, and it all went like clockwork as the iron road extended westward.

"This will be your post," Torn told Longshot. "Up here, at the head of the line. Scout from dawn till dusk. Keep your eyes open. Watch for any Coastal and Northern sharpshooters, and Indians, too. I'm going to make sure every crew is armed, if they aren't already, and I have no doubt they'll fight well, these Irishmen. Just try to keep them out of ambushes. Give them a fair chance, and they'll give a good accounting of themselves."

Longshot nodded happily. The task suited his talents. "And where will you be if I need to get word to you?"

"You and I can't do this alone. We need more good

men. Finding them will be my first priority. When I find them, I'll organize them into squads and post them at intervals along the line. Their job will be to patrol the rails and deal with any saboteurs who might have designs on the Great Western."

"Any idea where to look for these men?"

"I think I know right where to find them," replied Torn, but did not elaborate.

Longshot removed his paint from the boxcar stables. The two men shook hands and wished each other luck, and Torn boarded the private train to return to Whiskey Flat.

Finding Collie Rourke took a while. He asked Niles Keach where he might locate the leader of the Irish Brigade, and Keach told him Rourke was a hard man to track down.

"He isn't on the Great Western payroll anymore," said Keach. "Used to be, but when he took on the job of organizing the benevolent association, he quit. Said it wouldn't look right to the men he represented. Since he might have to stand up to the railroad, he couldn't very well have the railroad's money in his pocket."

"How does Bracken feel about him?"

"Collie's a real fire-eater. Cares intensely about the men and their working conditions. He's rough on the outside, but he has a big heart. The Great Western tolerates him because it has to. The Irishmen like him because they know he has their best interests at heart and he'll fight for what's right. So they're behind him all the way, and any disrespect shown him is taken personally by the whole bunch."

Torn remembered how the crowd had watched

him during his first confrontation with Collie
Rourke, in front of the Shamrock.

"Collie's fair-minded, too," Keach added. "There
haven't been any real big problems between the
Irish Brigade and the Great Western. Yet. None that
couldn't be worked out."

So the difficulty in locating Collie Rourke was that
he had his own agenda and could be anywhere. Torn
could do nothing more than ask around. He eventually found someone who informed him that Collie
and his "wrecking crew" were in Whiskey Flat.

"Wrecking crew?" asked Torn. He didn't like the
sound of that.

"Aye," said the railroader, with a broad wink. "Ta-
kin' care of business."

"What kind of business?"

But the Irishman was evasive. "Just lookin' out for
us paddies. That's what they do, Collie and his
crew."

Seeing that he would get no further information of
value from this source, Torn headed into Whiskey
Flat.

When he saw a crowd gathered in front of a raw-
board mercantile, he figured he had finally found
Collie Rourke. The man had a knack for creating a
scene.

A crash followed by a shout of alarm from within
the shebang caused Torn to quicken his stride.
Shouldering his way through the crowd, he stepped
in on a scene of imminent violence.

Collie and four brawny members of the Irish Brigade were on one side of a counter, and all but Collie
wielded clubs. A lone shopkeeper cowered on the
other side, his back pressed against a door. He had a
shotgun aimed at Collie and his boys. The merchant

was frightened, and his finger was on the scattergun's double trigger. A frightened man with a gun was the single most dangerous thing Torn could think of. But it didn't seem to faze Collie, who truculently stood his ground.

"Put that greener down, Henderson," growled Collie. "Else I'll make you eat the flamin' thing."

"You and your hooligans get out of my store, Rourke!" warned the shopkeeper.

"Put it down," snapped Collie, biting off the words. "If you don't, I'll—"

"You'll have a bellyful of double-ought if you make a move!" Henderson shouted.

Torn drew his Colt and aimed it at the shopkeeper.

"I'm going to count to three," he said very quietly. "And if by that time you haven't put that shotgun down, I'll kill you where you stand."

"But they come bargin' in here—"

"One."

"They got no right—"

"Two."

Henderson dropped the shotgun on the counter.

Collie grinned at Torn. "Why, Judge, I didn't know you cared."

Torn pushed through the Irish Brigade men to the counter. He holstered the Colt, picked up the shotgun, and turned to level the weapon at Collie and his boys.

Collie's grin vanished.

"Drop the clubs," said Torn.

"You don't understand. . . ." Collie began.

"Drop 'em."

"You're not making sense!" Collie fumed, turning

a deeper shade of crimson. "Whose side are you on?"

"I'm trying to keep the peace, Rourke. Trying to prevent a killing. You're making it damned difficult on both counts, you and your Irish Brigade."

"We're not outlaws."

"Then stop acting like you are."

Collie pointed an accusing finger at Henderson. "This man's running a flamin' opium den in that back room."

"First things first," said Torn.

"It's a dirty lie!" exclaimed the merchant.

"We'll see," said Torn.

Henderson made a run for it. With Torn holding the wrecking crew at bay, he saw his chance. Throwing open the door behind him, he bolted.

"After him, boys!" Collie yelled.

The Irish Brigade surged forward.

And pulled up short as Torn snapped the shotgun to his shoulder.

"He's getting away!" Collie complained.

Torn figured it was for the best. If Collie and his toughs got hold of Henderson with their clubs, murder might be the result. And he didn't want to hang these men if he could avoid it.

"You're about to run out of that notorious Irish luck," he said.

Collie Rourke took a long look at Torn and saw that this was so. The man in black was as hard and unyielding as stone. An altogether different proposition from Henderson. Collie had doubted that the shopkeeper had the nerve to shed blood. Torn had plenty of nerve, and to back down was not in his nature. He could not be bluffed or bullied. Collie had been willing to take his chances with Henderson.

But there was no chance against Torn, and Collie was smart enough to see that. His mission was righteous, but he realized that dead men seldom served their cause as well as the living.

"Come on, boys," he grumbled to the others. "I guess we know whose side the judge is on."

The scowling Irish Brigade shuffled out of the mercantile.

They were loitering out in the street, mingling with a crowd of about twenty other off-duty railroaders, when Torn emerged a few minutes later. The muttering ceased, and all eyes fastened on Torn.

"Two of your colleagues in that back room," said Torn. "Get 'em out before you tear the place down."

"What did you say?" asked an incredulous Collie Rourke.

Torn tossed the shotgun to Collie. Then he went back inside the store, returning to the street with an ax in either hand. These he gave to two members of the Irish Brigade.

"There's a barrel of those things inside. Knock this place down to the ground and then put a torch to it."

"What about the stuff inside?" asked a potential looter.

"No plunder," Torn warned sternly. "We're going to make an example out of Mr. Henderson. You're standing on the right side of the line, but if you stoop to looting, you step right over that line. Then you'll have to answer to me. And you don't want to have to do that."

"We don't want Henderson's stock anyway," Collie declared, addressing the crowd. "We just want him and his opium out of Whiskey Flat. What do you say, buckos? Is this shebang an eyesore?"

The men raised a cheer and surged forward.

Torn caught Collie's arm as Rourke swung past him to participate in the destruction. "When you're done here, I want to talk to you," he said.

"What about?"

"I need your help. The help of the Irish Brigade."

Collie squinted at Torn suspiciously. He wasn't sure he trusted him, or even if he liked the man.

Eventually, though, he nodded. "Aye," he said at last. "We'll talk."

"Good," said Torn, and moved on.

The enthusiastic Irishmen were well on their way to dismantling the raw-board building, and before Torn had walked a hundred yards, the place came crashing down. By the time he reached the rails of the Great Western on the northern rim of Whiskey Flat, what was left of the mercantile/opium den had been set ablaze. Ribbons of dense smoke were swept through the streets by a raw April wind.

To the denizens of the shanty hells who emerged into the light of day to find out what was going on, the smoke was an admonition.

Law—and the grim resolve needed to make it stick—had come to Whiskey Flat.

CHAPTER 13

"SURRENDERED?" SERGEANT GREGG GASPED.

He stared at Buck Drayton across the table in the remote soddy.

It couldn't be true. He couldn't believe his ears. He looked at the others. Tuttle and Bushrod were bandaged and laid up in their bunks, but Rosser and Brown and Underwood were here at the table. Their expressions, glum and a little ashamed, confirmed the unbelievable news.

"Drayton's Light Artillery ain't never surrendered," said Gregg.

"We have now," said Drayton flatly.

"To two men? You let two men capture the whole damned bunch of you?"

"That's enough, Sergeant."

Gregg stared at Drayton. "No, it ain't. What's got

into you, Cap'n? You ain't the same man we followed into all them scrapes. You've changed."

"Maybe I'm just getting tired," said Drayton, and he certainly sounded tired.

"We swore we'd never surrender after we heard about Appomattox, remember? Ain't that why we went all the way to Mexico back in sixty-five?"

Drayton drew a deep breath and made no reply. Gregg could not see in the man a glimmer of that fiery old defiance that had sustained him—hell, had sustained them all—through thick and thin all these years.

"What about Colonel Stinson?" asked the sergeant. "What's he gonna think?"

"He's a soldier. He'll understand. I accepted parole from Judge Torn."

"So what now?"

"Now? Nothing. Until we are released from our parole, we do nothing."

Gregg took a plug of tobacco from one pocket and a clasp knife from another. Cutting off a chew, he popped it into his mouth and worked on it awhile, staring morosely at the greenbacks on the table— the payment he had received from English Jack Gellhorn.

"Well," he said at length, "I warn't here, so I ain't surrendered, and I ain't paroled neither."

"Yes, you are. You're part of my command. You will honor my decision and obey my orders."

Gregg turned to the other men at the table.

"Well, boys, I never thought it would come down to this."

"Me neither," Rosser muttered.

Brown and Underwood just looked away.

"You all gonna just sit here like turtles on a log?"

Gregg asked. "Or are you gonna come along with me."

"Come along?" echoed a puzzled Rosser.

Gregg shook his head. "Private Rosser, you ain't got the sense God gave a chicken. I'm gonna take that Whitworth out yonder and I'm gonna bag me some more Great Western iron horses and make me some more Yankee money to spend on women and whiskey and such. Now that'll be a helluva job alone. I could use the help."

"But . . ."

"No buts about it, Private Rosser," snapped Gregg. "The cap'n here has decided he's tired of being a soldier. Fine. He can go raise taters somewheres and sit on a porch and watch the sunset for the rest of his life if he wants to. Me, I've always been a soldier, and I'll die a soldier."

"Then act like one," barked Drayton. Some of the old fire had suddenly reappeared in him. "God in heaven, Sergeant. I never thought I'd hear you talk this way. Listen to yourself! Don't you see what you're doing? You're inciting a mutiny."

"No, I ain't," said Gregg.

Drayton's right hand had been out of sight beneath the table. Now he brought it into view. He was holding a revolver in it, and he pointed the gun at Gregg.

"Christ," muttered Underwood.

Gregg looked down the barrel of the pistol with gruff disdain. "You ain't gonna shoot me, Buck," he said.

Drayton was pale. His lips were drawn thin.

"When we took an oath to the Confederacy, we took another oath as well. You remember that one, Sergeant? We swore our loyalty to the unit. Promised we'd stick together. You're breaking your solemn word."

"You surrendered!" Gregg exploded, slamming a fist on the table. "We swore an oath never to surrender, too, and you broke it."

"You're not taking my men or my cannon."

"You won't shoot," said Gregg. "Buck, your family and mine have been neighbors since our grandpas' time. Hell, Greggs and Draytons been fightin' together since the Creek War. And the Greggs sided with the Draytons, your pa and his brothers, when they was feudin' with them no-account Barrows. You couldn't pull that trigger if your life depended on it."

Buck Drayton's shoulders sagged. He put the gun down on the table and shut his eyes.

Smirking, Gregg stood up. "So what's it gonna be, boys?"

There was a moment's silence.

Rosser was the first to speak. "I'm sticking with the cap'n."

"Me, too," declared Underwood.

"I'll do the same," said Brown.

"Hell, Sarge," said Rosser, apologetic. "We been following the cap'n all over the place for nigh on sixteen years now. I wouldn't know what to do on my own stick."

"Yeah," agreed Brown. "We're old dogs. Too old to learn new tricks."

"You better just git," Rosser suggested. "And you can leave the Whitworth, if you don't mind. She may never get fired again, but I'm kinda attached to her. I'd miss her somethin' fierce."

Gregg was shocked by this turn of events. He stood there and stared.

Drayton opened his eyes. "Go on, Sergeant," he

said coldly. "Henceforth you will appear on the rolls as a deserter."

"To hell with you," snarled Gregg.

"Better git," Rosser said again.

"Fine," Gregg said resentfully. "I'll git. I'm going to do you boys one last favor, for old times' sake. I'm going to ride back to Whiskey Flat and find this Judge Torn you say you all got this parole from. And when I find him, I'm gonna shoot him down like the mangy dog he is."

Drayton rose. "No."

"You can't stop me."

"It won't make any difference, Sergeant. Don't be a fool."

"You're the damned fool, Buck. What do you think this is? A war? It ain't no war and we ain't soldiers no more. We're hired guns. Nothin' more nor less than that. Only thing is, we use a different kind of gun. Well, I'm still working for Colonel Stinson and the Coastal and Northern Railroad. And the way I see it, this judge is a bur under Stinson's saddle. So I reckon I'll just get rid of that bur. I followed you all over that godforsaken Mexico, Buck, because we was gettin' well paid to do other folks' fightin' for them. I'm in this for the money."

He snatched up the greenbacks and stalked out of the soddy.

Rosser stood, as though prepared to go after him.

"At ease, Private," said Drayton.

"If he goes gunnin' for that judge, they'll think we were all in on it," said Rosser. "They'll say we broke our word."

"I know," Drayton said miserably.

"So what are we gonna do, Cap'n?"

They were all watching him intently. Drayton

knew they were counting on him to make the right call. As they had always counted on him.

"I'll have to stop him," he said, and his voice was hollow.

"Beggin' your pardon for askin', Cap'n," said Brown, "but can you?"

Drayton knew it would be the hardest thing he had ever had to do.

But he could do it.

He picked up the revolver.

14

THE EXAMPLE SET BY THE IRISH BRIGADE, WITH TORN'S blessings, on the shopkeeper Henderson, seemed to have a salutary effect on Whiskey Flat. It was as though the denizens of the shanty hells were pulling in their horns a little—waiting and assessing this new element of law and order that had descended on them in the form of a federal judge.

For two days there were no incidents in the boomtown that could qualify as violent altercations between railroaders and vice purveyors. Folks claimed it was some kind of record. It was hard to believe— forty-eight hours passing by without somebody getting shot or knifed or at the very least busted up.

But it wasn't only Torn's presence that made the difference.

English Jack Gellhorn counseled tact and patience when other saloon and brothel owners came to him

—as most of them did—to voice their concerns and complaints regarding Judge Torn. Gellhorn listened patiently to them all—how they just couldn't let law and order get too solid a grip on Whiskey Flat, it was plain bad for business. English Jack would nod sympathetically and advise them to simply sit tight and wait. They left with the impression that he had already devised a plan of action for dealing with the judge.

In fact, Gellhorn himself was waiting—waiting for orders from Ezra Stinson. He had dispatched one of his men on a fast horse to take the news of Torn's arrival to the Coastal & Northern's head honcho. The way Gellhorn saw it, it was Stinson's call to make. He was running the show. English Jack was merely his secret agent. Personally Gellhorn hoped Stinson would pull strings with his cronies in the new Hayes Administration. Maybe they could arrange to have Torn removed. Or at the very least tie his hands and render him ineffective.

English Jack figured violence should always be the last resort. Not that he was a coward. Far from it. He was an excellent shot and good with his fists. He knew how to fight. But he thought it better business to use one's head to resolve a problem rather than one's fists.

When the messenger he had sent to Stinson returned with a note in a sealed envelope, Gellhorn discovered that the colonel did not have the same attitude.

The note read:

TAKE NO ACTION AGAINST TORN YOURSELF. YOU WOULD RISK

YOUR POSITION BY DOING SO. I AM SENDING SOMEONE TO

DEAL WITH THE MAN. HE IS A SPECIALIST IN THE FIELD OF
REMOVING OBSTACLES.

A specialist in the field of removing obstacles—
Gellhorn had a good laugh with that. Why was Stinson beating around the bush? English Jack knew exactly what kind of man Stinson was talking about.

A hired killer. No doubt, a gun artist.

Stinson was going to deal with Judge Torn the quick and easy way.

He was going to have him put six feet under.

Torn knew Whiskey Flat's good behavior was just a temporary thing, but he used the lull to good advantage.

He had his talk with Collie Rourke. The result was the organizing of the Irish Brigade into squads. Some of the squads rode the rails night and day, guarding against the possibility of Coastal & Northern sabotage. For this duty Torn tried to find men who had experience with explosives. Such men were not that hard to find.

Often these squads traveled by handcar. While Orly Bracken reluctantly consented to pay these men extra wages for hazardous duty, he would not— and claimed he could not—spare many locomotives for the service. Almost every Jupiter and Baldwin engine the Great Western owned was employed in shuttling supplies up to end-of-track as fast as was humanly possible.

The Great Western was making progress—three to seven miles of new track were being laid every day—and they needed every rail and cross tie they could get up there.

At this rate, Bracken crowed, they would make

Wolf Creek Pass in three weeks. "Maybe just your being here has made Stinson think twice," he said. "By the way, I like the way you handled that affair with the opium den."

"It was extreme," said Torn.

"Desperate times require desperate measures."

"Don't count Stinson out yet."

"Maybe he was counting on that damned rebel cannon to stop us for good."

Torn shook his head. Bracken was deluding himself if he thought a man like Ezra Stinson would give up after a single setback, or back down from a single man.

Personally he had a feeling all hell was about to break loose.

That night, after finishing dinner and having a brandy with Bracken and Niles Keach, he decided to take a stroll around Whiskey Flat and stated his intention of doing so. The Great Western's superintendent of construction thought it was a fine idea. Keach walked with him a ways before giving his opinion.

"It's like throwing kerosene on a fire," said Keach.

"What is?"

"You walking into town tonight."

"It's a free country."

"You know what I'm talking about."

Torn didn't say anything.

"It's like you're asking for trouble," Keach continued. "Whiskey Flat is a hornets' nest. You don't throw stones at a hornets' nest."

"This is my evening constitutional," Torn said wryly. "It helps the indigestion to take a stroll after supper. Makes you sleep better, too."

Keach grimaced. "That's pure horse puckey.

You're looking to stir up the water. I say it's better to leave well enough alone."

"Maybe I'll just go on over to the Shamrock and see if they have any bourbon."

"Bracken's got bourbon."

Torn pretended not to hear. "I could use one more drink before I turn in."

"Bracken's got bourbon," Keach persisted.

"Yeah, but I'm told English Jack Gellhorn peddles the best liquor in town. Care to join me?"

"No thanks. You can take care of yourself. Besides, I don't believe I'm in the mood for getting caught in a cross fire tonight, thanks just the same."

Keach stopped walking. Torn stopped, too, looking back to see Keach tilt his head in an attitude of intent listening.

"Listen to that," said Keach.

All Torn could hear was laughter and music and the thunder of bootheels from the dance halls. And then there was the whisper of the brittle-cold wind coming in off the plains.

"Listen to what?"

"No yelling. No gunshots. Ain't natural. Worries me. Whiskey Flat is a powder keg with a short fuse." Keach gave Torn a sharp look. "And you're the match, Judge."

"Good night, Niles."

Keach shook his head and trudged off, heading back in the direction of the iron road.

Torn bent his steps toward the Shamrock.

He could not know that at the very moment he stepped through the saloon's front door, Sergeant Gregg, late of Drayton's Horse Artillery, was slipping into Gellhorn's office through the back.

CHAPTER

15

WHEN HE WALKED INTO THE SHAMROCK, MANY HEADS turned, and Torn knew right away that in a few short days he had become something of a celebrity in Whiskey Flat.

He was used to this kind of attention. He wore no tin star, but he might as well have. As a federal judge, he was the symbol of law and order—even more so, perhaps, than many badge toters proved themselves to be. This was enhanced by his already legendary willingness to administer justice at gunpoint, or on the blade of his saber-knife.

The gamblers and dancehall girls, the bouncers and pickpockets—the whole legion of predators here to separate the railroad worker from his wages—looked at him with frosty reserve, if not outright animosity. Some of these made their living by illegal means, and it could be argued that the rest did so in unethical and immoral ways, and absolutely none of them were going to feel the least bit inclined to treat a federal judge, of all people, in a friendly manner. It was just the nature of things. He was on one side and they were on the other, and Torn actually preferred it that way.

As for the railroaders, they were only marginally less reserved in his presence. They liked the rough games they played—needed them as a release after long grueling hours of backbreaking labor—and even though they didn't have a nice word to say about the gamblers and had no respect for the girls, all of whom excelled in taking their money, they would have liked less not having the diversions of pokes and poker. The presence of this man in black, this steely-eyed symbol of law and order, was rain on their parade. They didn't want him around until they really needed him to set things straight.

Torn was not looking for friends. He had become a loner, and he liked it that way. He was prowling the shanty hells of Whiskey Flat just to make certain that his presence was felt—in other words, precisely for the purpose of raining on everybody's parade, just a little. By dint of past experience, he had learned that this policy usually served to keep the lid on the powder keg. Sometimes it backfired. That was what Niles Keach was afraid of. But Torn was accustomed to taking risks.

The seventy-five-foot bar was crowded. The paddies were two and three deep from one end to the other. But Torn wasn't deterred. He had a strong hankering for a shot of bonded bourbon. That was his drink of preference and he seldom came across the genuine article on the frontier. Plenty of watered-down red-eye and bathtub gin and tepid beer, but not the good stuff. And he figured if anybody in Whiskey Flat—aside from Orly Bracken—purveyed honest-to-goodness bourbon, it would be English Jack.

The men at the bar saw him coming, divined his intention, and parted to make room for him. It was a clear demonstration of the power of his reputation.

Gellhorn kept a half-dozen aprons working behind the mahogany every night, and even that platoon wasn't sufficient to wait on all the thirsty customers in a timely fashion. Some of the railroaders near the back of the crowd were impatient, but none of them begrudged Torn the ease with which he was able to belly up to the bar, or the alacrity with which one of the harried bartenders hustled over to wait on him.

Torn yelled his preference over the blare of the brass band and the cacophony issuing from the crowded dance floor. A moment later he found himself savoring the smooth bite of bonded bourbon, just what he had been hankering after. He didn't think it fair to monopolize the ten or so inches of bar space, so he stepped out of the crowd—and came face-to-face with the raven-haired woman he had seen on the train.

He was shocked to see her here, and made a quick assumption. She saw the surprise register on his lean, sun-dark features, and read the assumption in his eyes, and became immediately defensive.

"How do you do, Mr. Torn?"

"Fine," he said. "Rachel Bailey, isn't it?"

He looked her over, top to bottom, in a more brazen way than he would normally look at a woman. She wasn't dressed like a calico queen. No satin or silk, no lace or feathers, no war paint. She certainly didn't need the latter. Her beauty was flawless and natural. She wore a very respectable skirt and basque waist of blue serge. It was fashionable garb, if a little worn, and Torn found himself wondering about her. Obviously a lady of breeding, perhaps one who had fallen on hard times. But hard times or not, what was a lady of breeding doing in a place like this?

"Yes," she replied. "We met on the train."

It was a silly, useless statement—they both knew perfectly well where they had first seen each other. Torn realized they were skirting the issue, and it was a keenly uncomfortable situation to be in, so he stepped right into it.

"Is this where you were bound, Miss Bailey?"

"Yes. I came to find John Gellhorn." She said it with defiance.

His gaze darkened with disapproval. "I see."

"Oh, I don't believe you see at all, Mr. Torn," she flashed, more hurt than she cared to be by his disapproval. "If you will excuse me."

She left him, and he watched her vanish into the press of humanity, feeling none too proud of the way he had acted.

"Torn!"

He turned to see English Jack coming at him. There was urgency in Gellhorn's stride.

"Good God, man! What are you doing here?"

"Having a drink. I paid for it, by the way."

Apprehensive, Gellhorn glanced over his shoulder.

"You must leave."

"Pardon me?"

"Get out of here," Gellhorn snapped.

"Go to hell," Torn said cheerily.

"You don't understand. There is a man here who intends to—"

"Intends to do what?"

"Hey! British!"

Gellhorn whirled. Coming forward was a grizzled character wearing a ragged greatcoat. The man spat tobacco juice on the floor. He looked put out.

"I asked you where I could find this Judge Torn, Gellhorn," Sergeant Gregg said with reproach. "You ain't told me yet."

"I . . ." Gellhorn glanced sidelong at Torn.

Gregg's belligerent gaze locked onto Torn. "You the judge, mister?"

"Don't do it, Gregg!" Gellhorn yelled, hastily stepping backward.

Gellhorn's step back was all Torn needed to know about the situation.

English Jack was getting out of the line of fire.

An instant later Gregg was sweeping the greatcoat back and yanking a pistol clear of his belt.

CHAPTER 16

TORN WAS NO QUICK-DRAW ARTIST.

His greatest asset was one he shared with all gunfighters of any repute—the nerve to stand firm when hot lead started flying. In the end, this was the most essential ingredient of all. What mattered most in a gunfight was who shot more accurately. It mattered less who got the first shot off, especially if he sacrificed accuracy for speed.

In this instance it was Sergeant Gregg who fired first.

Torn was holding the shot glass, still half-full of bourbon, in his gun hand. He dropped it and reached for the Colt Peacemaker. But Gregg had already drawn his hogleg. There followed the flat percussive report Torn knew so well. The barrel of Gregg's pistol spewed smoke and flame.

Gregg's mistake was that he was still charging forward as he fired. He didn't think to stop and take careful aim. He was no gunhawk. His forte had always been the fieldpiece. His bullet splintered the bar behind Torn, having missed its intended target by inches.

Torn was the next to fire. He took better aim than Gregg had done, and his bullet struck the ex-Confederate, but not precisely where Torn had intended it to strike. For Gregg's shot had triggered pandemonium in the Shamrock. Up until the rebel sergeant's revolver had spoken, only a handful of people in the establishment, those who were nearest to Torn and Gregg, had been aware that an altercation involving lead slinging was in process.

After the first shot everybody in the place knew, and the reaction was predictable.

Everyone was moving, and in every direction. While many bolted for the door, jostling and shoving, others threw themselves to the floor. Men hollered and cursed; a woman screamed.

Few knew for certain where the shot had come from, and as a result, several men intent on vacating the premises inadvertently hurled themselves into the danger zone.

One of these collided with Sergeant Gregg. It was, if anything, a glancing blow, but enough to knock Gregg off balance at the precise instant when Torn, a second or two after Gregg's first shot, triggered the Colt Peacemaker.

The bullet that would have struck Gregg dead center in the chest caught the rebel artilleryman in the hip instead. The impact spun him halfway around. He grunted, winced, and fired again. But he had not yet fully recovered his balance. He was still reeling from the collision with one of English Jack's customers and the impact of the bullet from Torn's gun. This was one of the reasons he missed Torn a second time.

The other reason was that Torn had moved. Not much, merely to turn himself sideways. In this way he presented a somewhat smaller target for Gregg. He stood now in the classic duelist's stance. Raising the Colt, he extended his gun arm fully, which not only shortened the distance between the Peacemaker and Gregg, but also improved his aim. It was as he turned that Sergeant Gregg fired that second shot.

Having missed twice at fairly close range, and realizing belatedly that he had been hit, Gregg began to have second thoughts. Not about killing Torn—he was still as determined as ever in that regard, and perhaps now, with the man's lead in him, even more so. But he thought a different tactic might be wise. To stand toe to toe and blast it out with the gunslinging judge didn't seem to be working out right.

When he saw Torn lining up his second shot, Gregg acted fast. He grabbed the nearest innocent bystander. This happened to be the man who had bumped into him. It never occurred to the sergeant that this man had in a way saved his bacon. Gregg got a good solid hold on him with his left arm around his neck, and then whirled him around into the line of fire.

Gregg was no spring chicken. He had been the oldest man by far in Drayton's Light Horse Artillery. But grizzled though he was, he was still strong as an ox, and he didn't have any trouble at all manhandling the hapless railroader.

Torn's finger was squeezing the trigger. He came within a flea's hair of unintentionally shooting the railroader, letting up just in time, and swearing under his breath as he realized what Gregg was up to. The sergeant was using the befuddled Irishman as a human shield.

When he saw that this new tactic had worked—had prevented Torn from squeezing off a second shot—Gregg flashed an exultant grin and brought his pistol to bear a third time, lining up another shot.

This time he wasn't going to miss.

"I've got you dead to rights, you bastard!" he crowed.

"Sergeant!"

Gregg's head snapped around.

Buck Drayton was standing like a rock in the current of humanity streaming for the door.

He had his own pistol drawn and aimed.

"Drop the gun, Sergeant," Drayton ordered.

"You don't give me orders anymore," Gregg yelled, and turned his attention back to Torn.

He was sure Drayton wouldn't shoot.

Drayton's gun spoke.

A look of surprise frozen on his face, Sergeant Gregg dropped his pistol. The gun clattered on the sawdusted planks of the Shamrock's floor. Gregg followed, striking the floor with a dead thump.

The railroader shrugged his sack coat back square on his shoulder, tugged on his cuffs, and looked with remarkably cool disdain at the dead man at his feet.

"Sorry blighter," he said, and proceeded with slightly wounded dignity on his way.

The Shamrock was emptying fast. Most of those who remained were on the floor. Torn looked at Drayton. The ex-Confederate captain was staring bleakly at Gregg's corpse. Torn was able to put two and two together as well as the next man. He didn't need to be told what had led up to this shoot-out. He could make his own deductions.

He did not know Gregg, yet surmised that this had been the member of the Whitworth's gun crew he and Longshot had missed at the soddy. The one whose whereabouts Drayton refused to divulge. Gregg had come gunning for him, refusing to abide by Drayton's surrender of the unit. And Drayton had come to stop him. The captain had had no other recourse. Honor demanded it.

Torn turned his attention on Gellhorn.

He and Drayton and English Jack were just about the only ones left standing in the tent saloon. As shreds of gray gunsmoke swirled between them Torn's cold steely eyes met Gellhorn's, and narrowed.

English Jack felt a chill trickle down his spine.

He realized that Torn *knew*.

His own actions had given him away—had tied him inextricably to the ex-Rebels of Drayton's Horse Artillery, and by this association with Colonel Stinson and the Coastal & Northern. Could he talk his way out of it? Try as he might, he could not come up with a lie that would explain away this guilt by association. His usually facile mind failed him. He found it hard to think at all.

Because Torn had not holstered the Colt Peacemaker.

Pride rescued Gellhorn. He seemed to straighten up and stand almost regally, and a little defiantly. He slowly opened his clawhammer coat, to show Torn he was not "heeled."

Torn gave a curt nod and holstered the Colt.

Turning on his heel, he headed for the door to the street, pausing at Drayton's side.

"Come on, Captain."

Drayton followed him out of the Shamrock.

CHAPTER

17

"WHERE ARE YOU TAKING ME, TORN?" ASKED DRAY-ton. "To jail?"

"We don't have one in Whiskey Flat. And that would amount to rank ingratitude, wouldn't it?"

Drayton was in no mood for frivolity. He stopped walking. Torn turned, noticed that the captain was still holding his pistol, down by his side.

They stood in the street, and there was still quite a bit of commotion out in front of the Shamrock, so Torn motioned for Drayton to follow and moved into the deeper night shadows gathered between two tent cabins, one a barbershop, the other a dentist's office. Both were closed.

"You don't have to tell me what happened," said Torn. "I can figure it out for myself. And it's clear

Gellhorn has some kind of an association with Stinson."

Drayton watched him, tight-lipped, saying nothing. Clearly he was still of a mind to protect his former associates. Irritated, Torn shook his head.

"You're as stubborn as a mule, Captain," he said. "You still figure you owe Stinson your loyalty?"

"Yes."

"Then there's no point in asking you to join up with me and the Great Western."

"Certainly not," replied Drayton. He seemed to take the suggestion as an affront.

"You're on the wrong side of this."

"That's your opinion."

"Also happens to be true."

"No deal," said Drayton, adamant.

"Then go on. Get the hell out of here."

"That's a funny way to talk to a man who saved your life."

"Thanks."

Drayton started to turn away, stopped. "I have a question. Would you have just stood there and let Sergeant Gregg shoot you?"

"Well, I wasn't going to run. And I wasn't going to shoot through an innocent bystander."

Drayton gave him a long, appraising look, then started to walk away.

"Don't forget," called Torn. "You and your men are still on parole."

"I haven't forgotten," Drayton threw back over his shoulder.

When Torn got back to his private train, he found one of Orly Bracken's clerks waiting for him. The young man was huddled on the vestibule, shivering as the cold night wind swept across the sagebrush plains and through his thin coat and chilled him to the bone.

"Mr. Bracken wants to see you right away," he told Torn, teeth chattering. "He told me not to come back till I found you," he added, by way of explaining his vigil.

"You should have waited inside."

"Yes, sir. Maybe I should have," the clerk acknowledged. Way off out in the windy dark a coyote howled at the moon, and the clerk listened a moment to the mournful song. "But to tell you the truth, Judge, I was afraid you might come in later tonight and mistake me for somebody else and, well, ventilate me, sir."

Torn busted out laughing, but cut it short when he realized how serious the clerk was. Such was his reputation, then, that it made honest men afraid of him. That was a sobering realization.

They made their way to Bracken's Pullman. The Great Western's superintendent was pacing the floor in his private office. He was in a highly agitated state.

"Where the blazes have you been?" he barked.

"Whiskey Flat," said Torn, with asperity. He was a prideful man if nothing else, and he didn't much care for Bracken's imperious attitude. "I told you I was going into town when I left here."

"Yes, yes," said Bracken, with an impatient gesture. "I forgot. No matter. You're here now. We've got a problem up ahead. A big problem."

"What happened?"

"This came tonight, right after you left."

Bracken handed him a telegram.

Torn read:

> WORD FROM ARROYO GRANDE CAMP. ALL WORK ON BRIDGE
> STOPPED. MAN KILLED. FOREMAN AND PAYROLL GONE.

"That came from end-of-track," said Bracken, unnecessarily.

Torn nodded. The telegraph line kept pace with the railroad to facilitate communications up and down the line.

"What's the Arroyo Grande?"

"A damnably deep canyon we've got to span. Got a bridge crew camp set up there."

"I see." Then word had come to end-of-track by rider from the bridge crew camp and from there by wire to Bracken.

"I'm not sure what's happened," said Bracken. "You need to get up there and find out."

"Says right here what happened," Torn said grimly. "Who's the foreman?"

"Man named Moynihan."

"You know him?"

"Not personally. But I checked our records while waiting for you. We hired him over the winter. He used to work for the UP. Niles Keach vouched for him. Niles used to—"

"I know. So there's no connection between Moynihan and the Coastal and Northern?"

"None that we know of. My God, do you think he's one of Stinson's agents?"

Torn shrugged. "Could be. Or maybe he's acting on his own. If I catch him, I'll ask him."

"You mean *when* you catch him."

"So how bad is this?"

"Bad." Bracken sighed. "If all work has stopped, then it stopped yesterday. Arroyo Grande is less than ten miles from end-of-track."

"Bridge wasn't finished."

"No."

"Sounds serious."

"Damned bloody serious. It'll take you a day and a half to get there and get those men working again." The Great Western's superintendent shook his head morosely. "You can't lay track across the Arroyo Grande without a trestle, and it takes time to build a bridge, and our rail is just one day away from there. No way around the Arroyo Grande, either. You see the problem?"

"You're going to lose some time. How much depends on how close to finished the bridge is."

"Precious time," murmured Bracken. "Precious time. This may finish us, Torn."

"I better take some money along if you want those men to work."

Bracken winced. "Yes, dammit. And then catch Moynihan and get that payroll back. I'm assuming you will want to leave right away. I have wired ahead to clear the main track for you."

"I'll leave as soon as I find Collie Rourke."

"Rourke? What the hell for?"

"That bridge crew doesn't know me. I reckon it'll be a surly lot. These men will put up with bad food and working dawn to midnight and the hot sun and rattlesnakes and bad water, but they draw the line at not getting paid on time."

"What are you saying?"

"I'm saying they'll be in a real bad mood. They know Collie. Trust him. Maybe they'll listen to him."

"All right," said Bracken. "Find him, and then get to Arroyo Grande, double quick. Don't you see, Torn? Just a couple of days' delay and the Coastal and Northern beats us to Wolf Creek Pass."

"I see," said Torn.

CHAPTER

18

IT TOOK A PRECIOUS HOUR TO LOCATE COLLIE ROURKE. He was prowling Whiskey Flat with three burly Irish Brigade men. Having heard of the shooting at the Shamrock, he was expecting more trouble. Once they were under way on Torn's private train, bound for end-of-track as fast as the Jupiter could haul them, Torn told him what had happened at the Arroyo Grande camp.

"Aye," said Collie ruefully. "It has a smell to it, doesn't it?"

"How so?"

"I don't believe in coincidences, Your Honor."

"Don't call me that."

Collie flashed a mischievous grin. "As I was saying, it sounds to me like Coastal and Northern work."

He went to a window of the Pullman and looked

out at the night. "We're getting close to Wolf Creek Pass, and we were gaining ground on those beggars. Now this business at Arroyo Grande." He shook his head. "Perfect timing, for the Coastal and Northern. And too near by half, if you ask me."

"So you think Moynihan is one of Stinson's men."

"Well, I wouldna bet my grandmother on it, but then again, I wouldna be surprised. We'll find out, I s'pose, when we catch the blighter."

"I'll worry about tracking Moynihan down. Your job is to get that bridge crew back to work."

Collie nodded. "I'll do my best. But paddies can be stubborn as mules."

"You're living proof of that."

"Thank you. Your Honor."

Torn smiled. He was learning to appreciate the feisty Irishman.

He considered sharing with Collie his suspicions about English Jack Gellhorn—Gellhorn's apparent connection with Stinson and the Coastal & Northern by way of Drayton's Light Artillery—but thought better of it. One problem at a time.

A construction train delayed them; it was afternoon when they reached end-of-track. From there they went by horseback and wasted no time. Torn rode the Appaloosa Longshot had loaned him, and he had hustled up another cayuse back in Whiskey Flat for Collie's use.

He carried the payroll in a canvas and leather mailbag, the handles hooked over his saddle horn.

The days were growing warmer, and the ride proved to be a hot and dirty one. They followed the grade. Later today, Torn mused, the rails would be down along this stretch. In fact, by sundown the Great Western would be very close to Arroyo

Grande. How long would it take to finish the bridge, assuming they could coax the crew back to work? Would the Great Western lay any more track after today? Not without the bridge. As General Rhynes had said, no one needed a railroad that went nowhere.

Across the sagebrush desert they rode, with the mountains to the north a jagged blue line with white tips, seeming to float above the pale blue heat haze. They spotted a herd of fleet antelope and a few bison. Hundreds of meadowlarks flittered through the gray sage.

This splendid desolation moved Torn to bittersweet nostalgia, and he thought it odd that he felt that way—as though the wild country was already gone. Of course it was, really. In a dozen years he had seen great changes. He did not think they were for the good. He had watched the frontier dwindling, retreating before the relentless advance of civilization. Compared with the lurid squalor of places like Whiskey Flat, this arid, dusty plain was far more pleasing, not only to his eye but to his spirit.

Guilt stabbed at him, pricking his conscience. He realized he was playing a significant role in the demise of this country's natural state. Not just as the troubleshooter for a railroad—an iron road that would bring more people and more towns like Whiskey Flat to clutter these pristine plains—but in a broader sense as one of the men attempting to bring some semblance of law and order to a lawless frontier. Once that job was done, a horde of people would sweep across the land, consuming it. The buffalo and the antelope and the Indians would have to go. There would be no place for them anywhere.

Torn had come to love this wild, free, wide-open,

big-sky country—as much as he had ever loved the rolling hills and pine forests of piedmont South Carolina, and he was genuinely remorseful for the part he was playing in the death of it.

Collie turned out to be a lackluster horseman, so they made only fair time, and it was nigh on sunset when they reached the camp at the Arroyo Grande.

The camp consisted of about twenty tents, in two rows, not far from the rim of the canyon. Riding in, Torn could see part of the bridge trestle in the purple twilight. He could see piles of timber, wagons, a few horses in a rope corral as well. As for the bridge, he was no expert, but he thought there wasn't that much work left to do. So everything depended on the disposition of the crew, and Collie's ability to motivate them.

"Might be better if you hang back and let me handle this," Collie suggested.

Torn turned his attention to the men in camp. Some were sitting around fires in front of the tents. Others wandered aimlessly. Someone spotted them riding out of the gloom and gave a shout, and while more men emerged from the tents six grouped together and came forward to meet them.

"Welcoming committee," said Torn, and noticed that most of the men carried something in the way of a weapon—ax, sledgehammer, iron bar. He could feel the sullen animosity of the group.

"Don't look too friendly," said Collie.

"I'm not surprised."

"And they'll know you. Or at least they'll know who and what you represent when they see you and that Winchester and that Colt hogleg. They've been sitting around waiting for someone like you—someone from the railroad, sent to make 'em go back to work. One look and they'll make up their mind about you, and if you try to talk to them, they won't listen. It'll be like talking to a stone wall. You understand what I'm trying to tell you?"

"Yes," Torn said quietly. "That's why you're here. You talk them into finishing that bridge, Collie, and I'll watch your back."

"These are my people, Judge," said Collie, a little offended by what Torn was implying. "They won't raise a hand against me."

"You said it yourself. Moynihan was probably working for Stinson. How do you know there aren't more Coastal and Northern agents in this camp?"

Collie was silent a moment, considering this possibility. "Maybe you're right," he conceded.

"I hope I'm wrong," said Torn.

They rode a little farther. Fifty feet shy of the welcoming committee, Rourke dismounted. Torn handed him the mailbag containing the bridge crew's payroll and took charge of the reins of Collie's horse. Rourke walked on to confront the group.

The rest of the camp population—some thirty people, including a couple of women—were gathering behind the six whom Collie confronted, standing back a ways. Some of them carried lanterns. In the fast-fading light, Torn could not see beyond the limited reach of the lantern light as well as he would have liked. He was looking for firearms, but it was difficult to say who was armed and who was not. Still, it was clear that most of the inhabitants of the camp were content to be bystanders. They were close enough to hear what passed between Collie Rourke and the six men of the welcoming committee, but the fact that they were keeping their distance encouraged Torn to assume they would not intervene if the confrontation deteriorated into violence.

These foremost six, then, were the hotheads, the ringleaders of the strike. In any group, though, there was one who really did the leading. Torn scanned the six, and before the man had proven it by speaking first, the judge had picked out one individual as a likely candidate. He was a tall, broad-beamed, muscular man with the look of a pirate to him. This was due in part to the black patch over one eye, as well as the long mustache drooping down past his jawline and the bushy brows knitting together in a ferocious scowl.

Collie seemed to know him for what he was and said, "Well, Duffy, why am I not surprised? You always were one for stirring up trouble."

"The railroad's trying to cheat us, Collie," Duffy growled. "We won't stand for it."

"The Great Western?" Collie was surprised. "Way I heard it, your foreman stole the payroll."

"They can't pull the wool over our eyes. They put Moynihan up to it."

"That's flamin' crazy and you know it," said Collie. "The Great Western would have nothing to gain by such an act."

Duffy took a menacing step forward. He was carrying an ax and looked to be on the verge of raising it.

"You bloody traitor," he snarled. "So you sold out to the railroad, didja, Collie? You know what happens to traitors."

And he raised the ax.

CHAPTER 19

TORN DREW THE COLT PEACEMAKER AND FIRED.

The bullet kicked up dust between Duffy and Collie Rourke.

Duffy jumped back and glowered belligerently at Torn, squinting as he tried to see Torn better in the deepening gloom. Torn kicked the Appaloosa into motion and closed the gap, thumbing the Colt's hammer back.

"Don't make me kill you," he said flatly.

Duffy lowered the ax. He had no choice. That he had to back down didn't improve his disposition, and the crowd's mood seemed to take a turn for the worse. A hostile murmur rippled through the press of onlookers.

"Put the flamin' pistol away, Judge," said Collie.

Torn let the hammer down and leathered the Peacemaker.

He could see Collie's point. They were sitting on a powder keg, and any more gunplay might provoke an explosion that neither of them would survive. It wasn't certain that Duffy had really intended to cleave Collie in two with the ax. Conceivably he might only have been trying to intimidate Rourke. That was clearly what Collie had thought. He had stood his ground. Hadn't so much as flinched. But Torn hadn't taken that chance.

"So you brought a Great Western gunslick along." Duffy sneered.

"This is Clay Torn, federal judge."

"Aye, we've heard of him. Judge or not, he's still working for the damned railroad."

"Let's get one thing straight," Collie snapped. "The Great Western did not steal its own payroll. Judge Torn is here to pick up Moynihan's trail and hunt him down. I'm here to deliver this to you boys."

He held out the mailbag.

"What is it?" asked one of Duffy's henchmen.

"Another payroll."

This time the crowd murmur was considerably less hostile.

Torn kept his attention riveted to Duffy. The big man was scowling more fiercely than ever. This was clearly an unexpected development. No one had apparently considered the possibility that Bracken would be so quick to come up with more money. Everyone knew the superintendent was as tight-fisted as they came. Torn figured Bracken would have been less generous had the situation not been so desperate. As it stood, though, the second payroll threw a spanner into the mutinous works of Duffy and his followers. It wrenched the momentum over to Collie Rourke and the Great Western.

"That won't pay for Will Kelly's life," said Duffy. "He was my friend. Moynihan killed him. Stuck a knife in his back."

"If that's so, Moynihan will swing," said Torn.

"It's so!" Duffy yelled. "I'm saying it's so."

"It won't work, Duffy," said Collie. "Stand aside. You've had your day. The strike's over. We've got a bridge to build."

Duffy looked at his associates. No one seemed to know what to do. They were uncertain, on the defensive. They had been working the rest of the bridge crew with lies about the Great Western being behind the stealing of the payroll and the murder of Will Kelly, and now it was clear to all present that they had been lying.

Torn braced for trouble. This was the moment of truth. Either Duffy and his bunch backed down, or they tried one last desperate play. If one or more of them was an agent of the Coastal & Northern, then they would have to do something, anything, to keep that bridge from being finished.

Duffy took the mailbag.

Torn relaxed.

And then Duffy opened the bag, looked in it, and yelled, "It's a bloody trick!"

A curse roaring from his lips, he swung the mailbag, striking Collie and knocking him down. Then he flung the mailbag away and, straddling Rourke, raised the ax in both hands.

Torn kicked the Appaloosa as soon as Duffy yelled. The horse jumped forward, and Torn launched himself out of the saddle. The impact jarred the ax out of Duffy's grasp, and Torn's weight bore the man to the ground.

They rolled apart, jumped up simultaneously.

Duffy charged, letting loose a roundhouse swing. Torn ducked under and threw a punch into the man's breadbasket. It was like punching solid rock. Duffy wheezed, whirled, and closed in again. This time Torn feinted a body punch. Duffy dropped his guard, and Torn jabbed a right fist into his face. The blow staggered Duffy, snapping his head back. Torn saw an opportunity. He stepped in, threw two more punches, left and right. Both connected. But Duffy stayed on his feet. Torn swore under his breath and tried to back out, but Duffy grabbed him, snatched him clean off the ground, and then rolled him off a hip. Torn went sprawling, rolled, scrambled to his feet. Duffy was already after him.

And now he had a knife.

"I'm gonna cut you open and stomp on your guts," Duffy threatened, leering.

"Big mistake," said Torn, and reached under his coat.

Duffy lunged. Torn dodged sideways. The saber-knife clanged against Duffy's blade, a deft parry that drove Duffy off balance. The Irishman recovered, spun, struck again, wildly. Torn realized the man had little expertise in the art of knife fighting. Duffy was relying on brute strength rather than finesse. Torn, on the other hand, had learned to handle a blade as well as anyone on the frontier. He had fought some of the best blade men around. Some said he was as good as the legendary Jim Bowie had been. Torn didn't know about that, but he felt confident in a knife fight.

Duffy was overmatched. Introducing the knife was his downfall. Torn had resolved not to resort to gun or knife as long as Duffy confined the quarrel to fisticuffs. Even though this fair play put him at a distinct disadvantage with a man of Duffy's size. Now the advantage was Torn's.

He parried Duffy's stroke with ease, a quick circular motion that seemed to pluck the knife right out of the Irishman's hand. The blade went flying off into the darkness. Duffy stumbled forward, completely at Torn's mercy. Torn could have cut him open. Part of him wanted to—that dark, ruthless, vengeful part that had been with him ever since those terrible savage days at Point Lookout Prison. That dark side had first manifested itself the night Torn had made good his escape—the night he had run his tormentor, Karl Schmidt, through with the Yankee sergeant's own saber. Ever since then it had reared its ugly head now and again.

He caught himself in time and beat down that murderous red urge, that killing craze. Duffy didn't have to die. He was a big, bullying brute—very much like Karl Schmidt had been—and that was his sin.

So as Duffy stumbled forward, off balance, Torn transferred the saber-knife from right hand to left, balled his right into an iron-hard fist, and drove the fist downward, catching Duffy behind the ear. The blow dropped the Irishman. He was out cold.

Sensing more danger, Torn whirled. Two of Duffy's colleagues were lumbering forward, one swinging a sledgehammer, the other brandishing an iron bar.

Grinning like a wolf, Torn switched the saber-knife back to his right hand and made a come-on gesture with his left. "Want some scars to remember me by, boys?"

They hesitated. Looked at the hellfire in Torn's

eyes and then glanced uncertainly at each other. After that, they fixed their attention on the saber-knife.

Collie Rourke jumped into the breach. He picked up the mailbag and dumped the greenbacks out for everyone to see.

"No tricks!" he yelled. "Duffy was lyin' through his teeth. Can't you see?"

And of course they could see. The five men who had sided with Duffy knew they were in a tight fix. Two of them tried to make a run for it. The others stood pat and did not resist as the crowd surged forward to snatch them up roughly. The two who tried to flee were caught. It was all Collie could do to keep the irate crowd from beating their six captives to a pulp.

CHAPTER

20

DUFFY AND HIS HENCHMEN WERE TIED UP AND PUT together in one tent, under guard.

"Y'know," Collie told Torn, "some of those boys might not have known any better than to believe Duffy."

Torn nodded. He knew Collie meant the five who had backed Duffy up. "It's certain Duffy was in on it with Moynihan—another one of Stinson's agents. As for the others . . . well, we'll have to sort all that out later. For the time being, they stay tied up."

An hour later Niles Keach rode into camp. He pointed out the glow of huge fires lighting up the night on the eastern horizon.

"End-of-track," he said. "Just a few miles from here."

Torn had already seen the light—had already surmised that it issued from construction fires.

"We'll have the bridge up by noon day after tomorrow," promised Collie, having carefully surveyed the unfinished trestle.

Keach grimaced. "So we lose a day and a half. Puts us forty-odd miles behind. Would extra men speed the work?"

"You know it wouldna," said Collie. "They'd just be getting in each other's way, and we'd have rondo sports knocking their buckos into the arroyo."

Keach took a long look around the camp. "Things look peaceful enough. What happened?"

Torn told him what he knew. Keach was shocked and chagrined to learn that Stinson had infiltrated at least two men into the bridge crew.

"And how many more bad apples in the barrel? Last year he used dynamite and sharpshooters to slow us down. This year he's getting sly. So that's the way it's going to be. When are you going after Moynihan?"

"First light," said Torn.

"You've done a helluva job," said Keach. "Did more than I thought you'd be able to do. But this business here might be the last straw. I'm afraid the Coastal and Northern might beat us to Wolf Creek Pass on account of this delay."

"That kind of talk isn't like you, Niles," Collie rebuked. "You're no quitter."

Niles Keach shrugged wearily and without another word mounted up and rode back for end-of-track.

Torn sought out the mess tent to get a bite to eat. The Irishmen treated him with new respect, if for no other reason than that he had fought Duffy fair and square and beaten him—a feat few of them believed they could have accomplished if called upon to try. Still, it was respect mixed with reserve.

His belly full, Torn looked for a place to sleep and ended up in the tent once shared by two of Duffy's followers, who were now under guard in another part of the camp. He fell instantly asleep, dead tired after thirty-six hours on his feet, and faced by the unpleasant prospect of another long day tomorrow.

But early the next morning he got a pleasant surprise.

Longshot Gant rode into camp with a prisoner.

It was Moynihan.

Torn woke to a commotion outside his tent. He pulled on his boots, grabbed up his Colt, and stepped outside to see an angry mob encircling Longshot and Moynihan.

Both men were mounted. Moynihan's hands were tied behind his back, and the buckskin-clad hunter was leading his horse. The Irishmen were moving in on the hapless foreman, determined to drag him off his horse and do him great bodily harm. Longshot's shouts were lost in the tumultuous chorus of angry voices. Moynihan could do nothing but kick at his assailants. It was to no avail. They pulled him out of his saddle. Fists began to fly.

Torn shouldered his way roughly through the fringes of the crowd, but the crowd was too tightly pressed, and as a last resort he fired two rounds skyward.

The gunshots got everybody's attention.

"Get away from him," said Torn.

The crowd took one appraising look at him, remembering last night and what he had done to Duffy, and knowing he was deadly serious. Reluctantly they moved away from Moynihan. Torn took a position beside the fallen foreman. In a matter of seconds Moynihan had been beaten senseless. His face was a bloody mask.

"As long as I'm around," said Torn coldly, "you won't take the law into your own hands."

"He's a flamin' thief and a murderer," growled someone in the crowd.

"He's got to pay for killin' Will Kelly," declared another.

"He'll pay," said Torn. "But it'll be done by the book."

Collie Rourke appeared, half-dressed, thumbing suspenders onto his shoulders. He took one look at Moynihan, Torn, and the crowd, pieced it all together.

"Shame!" he cried, prowling around the circle of Irishmen. "You're all a discredit to the mothers who bore you. Beatin' a man whose hands are tied behind his back. Who canna defend himself. Shame on the lot of you!"

This fiery remonstrance took the steam out of the crowd. Feet were shuffled. Eyes were cast down.

"Now get on about your breakfast," Collie ordered sternly. "We've got a bloody bridge to build."

The mob, chastised, dispersed. Exasperated, Collie watched them go.

"Is it any wonder," he said to no one in particular, "that they think us uncivilized brutes?"

With that he tromped, scowling, after the bridge crew.

Longshot dismounted, shaking his head. "They caught me by surprise," he told Torn, apologetic. "I guess I should have known the minute I found this on that feller."

He removed a muslin sack from under his shirt and handed it to Torn. Torn knew without looking inside the sack that it had to be the stolen payroll.

"How did you happen to meet?"

"By accident. Just crossed trails. I started to ride up all friendly like. I knew Moynihan. Met him a few days ago. But he took a shot at me."

"And you didn't shoot back?"

"Sure I did." Longshot grinned. "That's one of my golden rules, Judge. Somebody takes a shot at me, I feel obliged to sling some lead at him in return."

Bewildered, Torn glanced at Moynihan. "Did you miss?"

"Shucks, no. Plucked the hat right off his head at about four hundred yards. He showed some sense after that. He didn't try to run, and he didn't try any more shooting, either. Just threw down his gun, threw up his hands, and began behavin' himself."

Torn smiled. "He must have heard why the Shoshones called you Longshot."

"Could be."

"Did he say anything? Tell you anything?"

"Not a word. But when I found the money on him, I figured he was up to no good. Thought I better haul him back over here and find out what happened. Guess I found out this morning."

Torn nodded. "He stole the payroll. May have killed a man in the process. Which way was he headed?"

"Due west."

"Toward the Coastal and Northern."

"Well, California's out that way, too, you know. What are you gettin' at? Don't tell me Moynihan worked for that scoundrel Stinson!"

"I'm beginning to think half of our crew does,"

Torn said dryly. "I had you swinging a wide loop looking for Indians and sharpshooters, when all along our trouble was right here in our own ranks."

"So what next?"

"Back to Whiskey Flat. English Jack Gellhorn works for Colonel Stinson, too. It's time to deal with him. Care to come along?"

"Sounds like fun."

Torn remembered Rachel Bailey, and the enamored way Longshot had looked at her when they met on the train. If there was going to be trouble over the woman, he thought he ought to find out early.

"There's something you ought to know," he told the hunter.

CHAPTER 21

It took a lot less time to make the return trip from Arroyo Grande to Whiskey Flat than it had to reach the bridge crew camp in the first place, for the simple reason that end-of-track was now only a few miles east of the canyon. Torn's private train was waiting for him. It created something of an obstacle for the construction trains hauling an unending stream of supplies up from the depots, but Torn had given specific orders to the engineer, and the latter had stuck faithfully to those instructions.

Torn and Longshot took Moynihan along with them. Collie Rourke was given the responsibility of delivering Duffy and his cohorts back to Whiskey Flat at a later date—as soon as he had finished supervising the construction of the trestle bridge. But Torn thought it wiser to remove Moynihan from the reach and wrath of the bridge crew. He wasn't sure but that those irate Irishmen might not decide to ignore his caveat regarding vigilante justice and deal violently with their erstwhile foreman. Collie's presence and influence alone might not be enough to guarantee their good behavior. Torn didn't want to hang the whole lot of them for murdering Moynihan. It was easier this way, removing the temptation.

Longshot was quiet all the way back to Whiskey Flat. Too quiet. Brooding. Torn's worst fears had been realized. The hunter had fallen head over heels for the pretty Rachel Bailey. And he was none too pleased to discover that she was consorting with the likes of English Jack.

"I want him alive," Torn had said. "I have reason to believe he's in cahoots with Stinson, and I want him to confess as much."

"What if he won't? You just gonna ask him politelike to fess up?" Longshot shook his head. "I guess you don't know the man very well."

"You do?"

"Much as I care to. He was taking those gandy dancers' money all last season. And in that time he went through about a half-dozen women."

"Look," said Torn, "you leave Gellhorn to me. I'll make him see it my way. And as for the woman, I didn't see your brand on her."

Longshot glared, thin-lipped.

But Torn didn't let up. "She told me herself she'd come out here for the express purpose of finding Jack Gellhorn. It's a free country, Gant, and she's entitled to make her own mistakes. What she does is her business and nobody else's."

"She needs to know what kind of man he is," Longshot insisted.

"Maybe she knows already. Maybe she doesn't

care. Maybe he's the kind of man she wants. And even if she doesn't know—even if she's got entirely the wrong idea about Gellhorn—it's not your place to interfere. She'll find out soon enough."

"When it's too late."

"Dammit," said Torn, exasperated. "She probably wouldn't believe you anyway. Some people want to be victims. Maybe she's one of those people."

"You're one cold-blooded hombre."

"And you're a fool, Longshot. Getting all starry-eyed over a woman you've been around for maybe a half hour, and maybe spoken twenty words to in your entire life."

"I think maybe I'm about through working for you, Judge."

"I thought you were a better man than that."

"I'm not tied down to this. We agreed."

"Yes, we agreed. You're free to go. But I have a feeling this business is coming to a head, Longshot. There'll come a day, and it's likely going to be soon, when I'll need you backing me up."

Longshot thought it over for a full minute. Then he shook his head. "I'm through," he declared resolutely.

"Fine. But don't get any ideas about gunning for English Jack. Don't make that mistake."

Again Longshot was silent. Ominously so, in Torn's opinion. He made no threats. That worried Torn. Men who talked big and tough and loud seldom followed their tall words with strong action. It was the men who didn't carry on about how they were going to do this or that who were the ones you had to watch.

* * *

They arrived in Whiskey Flat early that afternoon. The day had become overcast, threatening rain. Torn figured that was all the Great Western Railroad needed. As though it didn't have enough trouble, even the weather was conspiring against it.

Longshot took his leave without another word spoken. He went to the boxcar stables and removed both the paint and the Appaloosa. It was apparent Torn no longer had the loan of the Palouse. Torn made up his mind to confiscate Moynihan's horse—which was actually Great Western property—for the time being. As for Moynihan, Torn delivered him into the custody of an Irish Brigade squad.

His next stop was Orly Bracken's Pullman. The superintendent of construction was, as usual, behind his desk, buried behind a pile of ledgers. Three clerks were working feverishly in the outer office. There was a flurry of activity, a great deal of coming and going. Moving rails and ties and other supplies and fresh work crews up to end-of-track was a logistical nightmare, and nobody seemed to be having a good time.

But Bracken's dour face lit up when Torn tossed the stolen payroll on top of the ledgers. "Niles Keach telegraphed me that you had gotten things under control at Arroyo Grande. But he didn't say you had nabbed Moynihan."

"Longshot Gant brought him in."

"Good, good. Where is he?"

"Safe and sound. He'll get a fair trial, when I have time to see to it."

Eyes glittering, Bracken leaned forward. "Did Stinson put him up to it?"

"I haven't asked him. But I will."

"Think he'll talk?"

Torn shrugged.

"My God, if he would implicate Stinson!"

"I'll try to make him a deal he can't refuse."

"What kind of deal?"

"He may have murdered a man up at Arroyo Grande while escaping with the payroll. The best I could do is give him life in prison, as an alternative to the hangman's noose."

"I see." Bracken lost some of his enthusiasm. "Then you don't have much room to work."

"If he won't talk, maybe Jack Gellhorn will."

Bracken's jaw dropped. "English Jack? You mean . . . ?"

Torn nodded.

"How long have you known?"

Torn told him about the ex-Confederate named Gregg and his affiliation with Gellhorn. "But I had to take care of that business up at Arroyo Grande first," he added.

"Christ!" breathed Bracken, aghast. "You mean Gellhorn has been working for the Coastal and Northern all this time?"

"Probably from the get-go. Stinson couldn't have recruited a better man. He's in a perfect position to make trouble for you and your men. He hears everything at the Shamrock. Knows everything. If he sees a chance, he can lure some of your Irishmen off the straight and narrow. And he can serve as middleman between Stinson and Stinson's agents—men like Moynihan."

"How did he come to throw in with Stinson?"

"I don't know. I'll ask him."

"You're going after him now?"

"Right now."

"I've heard he's a crack shot. Rumor has it he was

drummed out of the British army for fighting a duel."

"I fought one of those, too," said Torn grimly. "A long time ago."

"When you were a young cavalier in South Carolina, I'll warrant." Bracken smiled at Torn's surprise. "I've heard some rumors about you, too, Judge."

"Well, I hope this doesn't boil down to a duel."

"I'd put money on it," was Bracken's ominous reply.

WHEN TORN WALKED INTO THE SHAMROCK, IT WAS THE middle of the afternoon; even so, the saloon was doing a fairly brisk business. In its race to beat the Coastal & Northern to Wolf Creek Pass, the Great Western was working on the iron road round the clock, with full crews changing over on eight-hour shifts. As a result, there were plenty of off-duty railroaders with money burning holes in their pockets at any hour of the day or night.

Torn looked for Longshot first thing, and wasn't too surprised to see him. The hunter was leaning against the portable bar. He wasn't drinking. The Sharps buffalo gun was tilted against the bar beside him. He had his back to the door and he didn't see Torn enter. He was staring at English Jack Gellhorn and Rachel Bailey, who sat at a table at the very rear of the saloon, playing cards. Neither of them, apparently, had noticed Longshot, or if they had, his presence had meant nothing to either one of them.

As usual, Torn's arrival put a damper on the Shamrock's crew and clientele. By now everybody had heard about the shooting of two nights previous, and when Torn stepped into the saloon, death strolled in alongside him. People ceased drinking, gambling, and dancing. Everybody stopped what they were doing and stared. It started at the front—this tense immobility—and spread to every corner like a wildfire.

Gellhorn and Rachel heard it, felt it. They looked up from the pasteboards. The only person it seemed not to effect was Longshot. He leaned against the bar, as motionless as a wooden Indian, like a man in a trance, and his gaze never strayed from that table in the very back.

Torn walked up beside him. As he neared the bar the men on either side of Longshot discreetly removed themselves. It was this that finally brought Gant to his senses. He looked around, saw Torn, and his expression became as bleak as a high-country winter.

"You have two choices," said Torn. "Either you back me up or you get out."

"This is a free country. You said so yourself."

"I have reason to believe you are contemplating murder," said Torn.

"You going to arrest me?"

"Do I have to?"

Longshot glanced at the Sharps Leadslinger.

Torn made up his mind that if Gant touched the rifle, he would draw the Colt and try to lay the man out cold. He didn't want to have to shoot. That was the last thing he wanted. But Longshot was acting crazy. There was no telling what he might do.

But Longshot didn't reach for the buffalo gun. "I'll back you," he said, his voice hollow.

Torn hesitated. Could he trust Longshot? He knew he could not. Gant was irrational. Still, he had given the man a choice. He couldn't renege now.

"Remember one thing," he warned. "I'll do the talking. You stay out of it."

"Sure."

"I don't want any killing done, if it can be avoided."

"That's up to Gellhorn, isn't it?"

"Yes. It's not up to you."

Longshot nodded.

Torn took a deep breath and walked the length of the Shamrock to Gellhorn's private table. Longshot picked up the Sharps and followed in his wake. He stood off to one side, the buffalo gun cradled in the crook of his arm. Rachel Bailey gave the lanky hunter a long look. English Jack merely glanced at Longshot and looked curiously at Torn.

"Good afternoon, Judge. I understand there was a spot of trouble up at Arroyo Grande."

"You should know."

Gellhorn refused to be baited. His smile was faintly condescending. "One of the advantages of being a saloon keeper. I hear things."

"You knew about this before it happened."

"I'm sure I haven't the foggiest idea what you are referring to."

"You made a big mistake."

"Did I?"

"The other night. I know all about you. So you can quit playing games."

Gellhorn's smile vanished. "Ah. You must be referring to the late, unlamented Sergeant Gregg."

"You knew Gregg had come gunning for me. How

did you know? Because he told you. Why would he tell you? Because the two of you were on the same side. Working for the same man. Stinson."

"You haven't a shred of evidence to substantiate such a claim."

"I don't have to prove it," Torn said softly, leaning forward, knuckles on the table. "All I have to do is tell these Irishmen."

"Assuming they would believe you."

"Want to find out?"

Gellhorn glanced beyond Torn. Torn didn't have to turn and look to know that every person in the place was watching them. The Shamrock was as silent as a tomb.

English Jack realized Torn was right. He did not have a single friend among the ranks of the Irish paddies who worked the iron road. They would be willing to believe any story, substantiated or not. They would not need much of an excuse to tear the Shamrock down to the ground and bury him under the rubble.

He sat back and flashed a wan smile that was supposed to be reassuring at Rachel Bailey. "Don't worry, my dear. Really, Judge. Where are your manners? This is scarcely the kind of talk to indulge in, in the presence of a lady."

Torn wasn't fooled. He kept his eyes on Gellhorn. It was a shyster's game English Jack was trying to pull on him. He was hoping to divert Torn's attention to Rachel. But Torn was watching, and he saw Gellhorn's hand move. English Jack realized he had failed and hooked a thumb in the watch pocket of his vest.

"Both hands on the table," said Torn.

Gellhorn obeyed. That condescending smile was back.

"Don't you trust me?"

"I'm betting you have a gun under that coat."

"If so, go ahead and reach for it," Longshot suggested.

"What's your stake in this?" Gellhorn asked the hunter.

"I just don't like you."

"That's enough," said Torn. "English Jack, you're too smart to make a dumb play like that."

Again Gellhorn glanced at Rachel. "You see, my dear. As in poker, so, too, in life. When the odds are too high, all you can do is fold."

CHAPTER 23

"THAT'S RIGHT," SAID TORN. "NEVER DRAW TO AN inside straight. Especially when the deck is stacked against you."

"Indeed." Gellhorn turned his attention back to Longshot. "What have I done to you, sir, that you ache so badly to kill me?"

Longshot's eyes were on Rachel. He didn't have to say anything in reply. Gellhorn could read the truth —it was written all over his face. So could Rachel. English Jack looked amused. She looked surprised.

"So that's it," said Gellhorn. "You have another admirer, my dear Rachel."

"She's not yours," said Longshot. "Are you, ma'am?"

"Just stay out of it, Mr. Gant. Please."

"I am heeled, as they say, Judge," English Jack

confessed. "You see, I was rather expecting this visit."

Torn nodded. "You gave yourself away with that Sergeant Gregg. He came to kill me, I guess, because I put the Drayton Horse Artillery out of commission."

"He was rather irate. You see, Sergeant Gregg wanted to make a lot of money killing iron horses. I suppose he blamed you for making that impossible."

"You didn't want him to shoot. But I know it wasn't for my sake."

"Not really, old chap. Awfully sorry. But as I always say, blood is bad for business."

"I've heard you were a duelist."

"Yes. I fought a duel. And you see where it got me. This godforsaken frontier. But guns are a poor substitute for brains."

Torn pulled out a chair and sat down across the table from the Englishman. "Are you still wanted by the British army?"

"Quite. I might have faced a firing squad. So I deserted. But you won't be turning me over to the British army, will you, Judge?"

"That's what I mean. You're smart. Too smart to go for that pistol under your coat. And, hopefully, smart enough to cut a deal."

"No, I don't think so. That wouldn't be smart."

"Why not?"

"Because I know Colonel Stinson."

"How did that happen?"

Gellhorn chuckled. Torn admired his presence of mind. The man was in a tight spot, but he was keeping his wits about him.

"I'm sorry. I really can't tell you about that. Stinson would be most unhappy. Now, there is a man who believes in violence as the cure for every ailment."

"So you won't tell me."

"If I did, what would you do?"

"Make out a warrant for his arrest."

"And serve it personally, I'd wager."

"Of course."

"Stinson has powerful friends in the new administration, Judge."

Torn shrugged. "If men like Stinson are above the law, then they can have my job."

"I rather like you, Torn, I must confess. I wish we had met under different circumstances."

"Wouldn't have changed things. We'd still be on different sides."

"Perhaps."

"You figure Stinson would come after you if you talked? You'd be in my custody. Under my protection."

Gellhorn laughed. "For what that's worth. No offense, but it isn't worth much. Not against a man with Stinson's money and connections. I will tell you one thing, Judge. Because I like you. Stinson is sending someone to deal with you. A specialist. I believe that's the word Stinson used."

"A paid killer."

"An assassin, if you will."

"Who?"

"That I honestly don't know."

Torn sighed. "Well, first things first. I'm going to close you down, English Jack."

"I expected as much." Gellhorn looked at Rachel. "Don't be alarmed, my dear. I will make certain you are well provided for."

"That's not your place," said Longshot. "Besides, it's a lie."

Gellhorn's eyes flashed anger. But he kept his emotions in check.

"I've got Moynihan, by the way," Torn told him.

He threw the name out just to get a reaction. It was a ploy, but it worked. A flicker of alarm crossed English Jack's features. Enough to tell Torn that there was a connection between Gellhorn and the errant bridge crew foreman. As, no doubt, there was a connection between English Jack and a great many of the mishaps that had befallen the Great Western.

Having gone out on a limb, and finding it stronger than he had expected, Torn went a little farther. "I know most of it," he said. "You're the middleman. Stinson's liaison with his agents. They report to you, you report to Stinson. And you relay his instructions to them. Isn't that about the way it works?"

"My humblest apologies, but if I told you any more, the next hired killer Colonel Stinson dispatched would be coming for me."

"You're under arrest," said Torn flatly. "Slowly, with the thumb and forefinger, bring the gun out and lay it on the table."

Gellhorn did as he was told, aware that Longshot was watching him like a hawk, and knowing that the hunter was praying he made a sudden move.

"Porterhouse," said English Jack, referring to the pistol. "Caliber thirty-eight."

Torn stood up. "Let's go."

Gellhorn rose, shot his cuffs.

"Will any of your men try to stop me from taking you out of here?" Torn asked.

English Jack surveyed the silent crowd. "I rather

doubt it. Like rats, they have deserted a sinking ship. I daresay they are more leery of you than they are of me. Shall we go?"

Dignified, he came around the table.

Rachel reached for the gun on the table.

"No!" yelled Longshot, and moved.

She fired the Porterhouse.

The bullet caught Gellhorn in the back of the head. He pitched violently forward in a spray of crimson blood and gray matter, and was dead before he hit the ground.

Torn drew his Colt Peacemaker. Longshot was still moving toward her. But Rachel backed away and dropped the Porterhouse as though it scorched her fingers, and did so before Longshot could reach her or Torn could level the Colt at her.

The hunter drew up short. "God in heaven," he breathed, horrified. "Why?"

Torn thought that one word, wrenched out of Gant's throat, reeked of broken dreams and despair.

Her beautiful face a pale stony mask, Rachel Bailey stared at her gruesome handiwork. "I told you I came looking for him," she said.

Torn realized she had indeed told him that very thing. He waited, knowing the rest would come.

"He killed my sister."

"Gellhorn?" Torn found that hard to believe. English Jack had been a lot of things, but . . .

"Oh, he didn't pull the trigger. She did. She killed herself. Because of him. He never knew about that. Not that he would have cared. He wouldn't have lost any sleep over it. Not him.

"You see, it didn't matter at all to him that she had fallen in love with him. He laughed at love. They met in Philadelphia. That's where I'm from, Mr. Torn. I never saw him until a few days ago. But I could see what an effect he had on her. He cast a spell over her. I know of no other way to describe it. He wasn't in Philadelphia very long. He was on his way out west. She soon followed him. Much against our father's wishes, I might add.

"Months later I received a letter from her. She was in Dodge City. The letter was full of despair. He had promised to marry her, but of course he never had any intention of delivering on that promise. When he grew tired of her, he left again. This time he made sure she understood that she wasn't welcome to follow.

"I wrote her back. Begged her to come home. Sent her enough money to make the trip. And I pleaded with Father to write her, too. To tell her that he forgave her. I felt that would make all the difference. I wasn't sure she would come home unless Father made an overture. She was too ashamed. But Father is a hard man. He said Gellhorn was nothing but a scoundrel, and that Elizabeth had shamed the entire family by her foolish actions."

Tears glistened suddenly in Rachel's eyes as, finally, she looked up at Torn.

"A few weeks later we received the news. She had committed suicide. Oh, Mr. Torn, can you imagine what that did to Father? The guilt broke him. He has not been the same since. He will never fully recover from the blow. He refused to forgive her, and now it's too late."

Torn glanced at Longshot.

"Gant, I've got to place her under arrest. Are you going to stand in my way?"

Longshot stared at her a moment longer. "No," he said, his voice hoarse and bleak and lonely.

And he turned to walk out of the Shamrock.

Torn never saw him again.

CHAPTER 24

WITH THE BRIDGE ACROSS ARROYO GRANDE FINISHED, the Great Western surged northwest, making for the Rockies.

The Irish toiled to lay iron, consuming the steady stream of rails and ties being rushed forward to end-of-track. It took forty cars of matériel for every mile of road. Six hundred tons of it. Fifty miles and more ahead, two thousand graders began to tackle the dusty foothills of the mountains, sculpting cuts and fills. Up into the forests went the timber gangs, and down the rivers and on wagon trains came the ties. Along the iron road itself came Niles Keach's contracted iron. He worked twenty hours and more a day to make sure Bracken got all the rails he needed.

It rained, but the rain could not slow the Great Western now. Then came the heat, more heat than was common for late April. It seemed as though Mother Nature was bound and determined to use every weapon at her command to stop the railroad. One week two men died every day from sunstroke. On top of that there were deaths from dysentery, deaths from gunshot, deaths from rattlesnake and Gila monster, deaths from senseless accidents in all the reckless rush. But none of it stopped the Great Western. The dusty graves were akin to mile markers. Such was the human cost of building the iron road.

The boarding train crept forward, carrying its thousands of paddies, and Whiskey Flat was left behind. Without the Irishmen's money, the town was doomed. The saloon owners and merchants and gamblers and calico queens gathered their plunder, struck their tents, and moved on up the road.

A new boomtown appeared one day in the foothills. They called it Sidewinder, for on the very first day of its existence a bartender was struck down by a rattlesnake. His was the first grave, but not the last, in the town's boot hill.

And Whiskey Flat became as it had been before: alkali dust and sagebrush, with human debris added for bad measure. No one seemed inclined to stay and make a go of it. All that remained were two dozen graves.

At night, when once one would have heard the strident call of the spielers and the thunder of boots on the dancehall floors and the shrill cackling laughter of some painted harridan, and maybe a gunshot or two—now there was only the sharp cry of a coyote as it dug through the rubbish heaps and the rumble of a construction train trundling by on the iron road and the whisper of the desert wind as it

pushed tumbleweed across the final resting places of
English Jack Gellhorn, late of the Royal Fusiliers,
and of Sergeant Gregg, born in Tennessee, dead in
Colorado, late of Drayton's celebrated and long-lived
Light Horse Artillery, CSA.

That same night, thirty-five miles away in Sidewinder, there was the boot thunder and laughter and
spiels, the slap of pasteboards on green baize, the
chink of poker chips and hard money, the clink of
shot glasses and whiskey bottles, the occasional gunshot, drunken angry shouts of the more frequent
brawl, the effluvium of tobacco smoke and bad whiskey and a thousand sweaty Irishmen—all of it bounc-
ing off the slopes of the foothills and rising up into
the purple star-studded sky, while the snowfields
above the timberline on the rugged, looming peaks
looked down, majestic and aloof and untouchable.

There was one thing missing in Sidewinder. The
Shamrock. It had been a fixture in Whiskey Flat and
a half-dozen previous end-of-track boomtowns. The
other saloon owners split the Shamrock among
themselves, lock, stock, and barrel. The girls went to
work for someone else. So did the bouncers and the
gamblers and aprons. Even the pickpockets found
new sponsors. The Shamrock's vaunted supply of
bonded whiskey was split up and watered down. No
one had room for Gellhorn's unique portable bar, so
its two halves were separated and never got back
together again, becoming instead part of the decor
of two rival watering holes. The big canvas circus
tent was likewise shared. The Shamrock was thoroughly cannibalized. There was nothing left.

Eight days from Arroyo Grande, as the steel
reached the foothills, the Kiowas made their long-
awaited appearance, swarming suddenly out of a

coulee on fast, shaggy mustangs, yipping and shooting and darting around a steel gang like pesky mos-
quitoes. Torn was not present at the fight, but he
had arranged for all the crews to have plenty of firearms near at hand.

As he had predicted to Longshot Gant, the Irishmen acquitted themselves in an admirable fashion.
They laid down their tools, picked up their carbines,
took cover behind the grade, and started shooting
back.

The fight was furious, but brief. There was a lot of
dust and excitement, but not much bloodshed. A
couple of Kiowa braves were slain. An Irishman was
wounded. The Indians realized they were outgunned
and soon retreated. Then the paddies put their guns
down, picked up their tools, and went back to work,
as though a Kiowa raid was just an everyday thing,
nothing to get worked up over.

The paddies worked like men possessed. The
word was out. They were in a race, and they wanted
to beat the Coastal & Northern. There was a fever.
An urge to win. Everybody seemed to be in a hurry.
It wasn't the result of anything said by Bracken or
Keach or Rourke—no encouraging words passed
down through the crew foremen from the big au-
gurs, or spread through the Irish Brigade members
from the leader of the benevolent association. It just
happened. Pride was the motivation. Pride made the
Irishmen work as though every one of them had a
share in the Great Western and would get rich if the
railroad beat Stinson's road to Wolf Creek Pass.

And then there was pride as well in being Irish.
The men wanted to show what they could do. They
had heard that the Coastal & Northern was using

coolie labor, and no Irishman wanted to be second best to a Chinaman.

Higher climbed the iron road into the foothills. A hundred supply trains racketed along the rails, belching black smoke. The men worked fast, and crews came along to clean up the road; quality mattered less now than quantity—the number of miles they could put down in a day. Three miles was the average at first, then four, and one day they put down almost seven miles of new road. That in itself was quite an accomplishment.

The men labored and some died, but they would not slow down for anything.

Torn decided he had never seen better men. What chance did the mountains have to withstand such men as these?

CHAPTER 25

ORLY BRACKEN MOVED HIS PULLMAN HEADQUARTERS UP to Sidewinder, and it was in Sidewinder that Torn spent most of his time for ten days following the killing of English Jack Gellhorn.

The closer the Great Western got to Wolf Creek Pass, the more nervous Bracken became. He fully expected more dirty tricks from Colonel Stinson, and he seldom let an opportunity pass him by to query Torn about any signs of further underhanded activity that could conceivably be the handiwork of the Coastal & Northern.

So it was that one evening, when Torn received a summons from the railroad's superintendent, he figured he was going to get grilled again by the paranoid Bracken.

In fact, Bracken's first words were: "Any trouble out there?"

Torn shook his head. "Things have been fairly quiet of late, apart from the usual daily brawl."

"No sabotage? No sniping from the hills at our work crews? Nothing?" Bracken sounded suspicious, as though he suspected Torn of withholding information.

"None that I know of. Collie Rourke and his Irish Brigade are doing a fine job patrolling your road."

"Nice to know they're good for something," was Bracken's caustic reply. He was loath to admit that Collie and his fellow members of the benevolent association were in any way beneficial to the railroad, or that the railroad owed them thanks. After all, strictly speaking, Collie and Bracken stood on opposite sides of the labor–management dispute, and Bracken still suspected that the Irish Brigade had inherited the mantle of the Molly Maguires.

"Collie Rourke's a good man," said Torn, determined to see credit given where it was due.

Bracken sniffed, and changed the subject. "It's too quiet, Judge. Things are going along too smoothly."

Torn smiled. This sentiment was to be expected from a man who had fought tooth and nail to overcome one obstacle after another to get his job done. Bracken was leery of smooth sailing precisely because he wasn't accustomed to it.

"Enjoy it," Torn advised.

"But what's Stinson got up his sleeve?"

"Maybe nothing."

"You're saying he just gave up trying to stop us?" Bracken shook his head emphatically. "I don't buy that. Not Stinson."

"He probably thinks he's done enough. Maybe he's convinced the Coastal and Northern can win the race to Wolf Creek Pass without his having to indulge in any more foul play."

Bracken grunted skeptically. "Well, I've sent a man out to check on the Coastal and Northern's progress."

"It's going to be close," predicted Torn.

"Sounds to me like you think your job is about done here."

"I was sent to make sure you got a fair chance."

"And you did a good job. I commend you for it. I have to admit, I had my doubts about you at first."

"I think I'll stick around a little longer, though. At least until we reach the pass."

"I see," said Bracken, suddenly noncommittal.

"And what if Stinson does beat you there? What will you do?"

"I know what you're driving at. You're wondering if there will be a battle for the pass."

"One way or the other, yes."

"I'm not Stinson. If the Coastal and Northern reaches the pass first, then the Great Western loses. It will be finished. We will have lost."

"You won't try to take the pass by force?"

Slumped in a chair behind his cluttered desk, Bracken grimaced. The prospect of defeat was not pleasant to contemplate.

"No," he said gruffly. "I won't stoop to Stinson's level. But if we reach the pass before the Coastal and Northern, and Stinson tries to take it from us, then we will fight."

Torn nodded.

"I have been wondering why you haven't arrested Colonel Stinson," said Bracken.

"I don't have any evidence."

"What about Moynihan?"

"He won't talk. If he does, he signs his own death warrant. Or so he is firmly convinced."

"Probably right. Stinson would stop at nothing to silence him. I've never met a more despicable, unprincipled man."

"Even if Moynihan did talk, you've still got to think Stinson would come out of it free and clear. His high-priced lawyers would convince a jury that Moynihan was just trying to save his own skin. There's no solid evidence connecting him to Stinson. My only hope for evidence died with English Jack Gellhorn."

Bracken sat up straight. Mention of Gellhorn reminded him of Rachel Bailey.

"I'd forgotten, but General Rhynes received a telegram from Philadelphia the other day. It concerned your prisoner, Miss Bailey."

Torn wasn't surprised. The sensational murder of English Jack had brought the news hounds out of the woodwork. Several frontier correspondents had pestered him for the lurid details of the shooting. It was the kind of story Eastern newspapers hungered for. Scandal and vengeance sold, these days.

He had not cooperated, but he had known his reticence would make no difference. The correspondents had gotten their story, and the story would be blazoned on the front pages of the scandal sheets.

"Her father, I reckon," said Torn.

"It seems Mr. Thomas Bailey is a very influential man. He very much desires—"

Torn held up a hand. "Don't tell me. I know. He lost one daughter by his stubborn, unforgiving silence. He wants to make amends by saving his other daughter from the scaffold."

"Surely you don't think Miss Bailey would hang."

"Once upon a time I thought that was up to a jury."

Bracken's chuckle was a dry rasp. "No, you're not that naive."

"So what does the general want to do?"

"He wants to know your intentions."

"No orders?"

"He told you at the beginning, Judge. You would answer to no one."

"So he's leaving it up to me?"

"Essentially, yes."

"I bet that's not what he told Mr. Bailey."

"I have no idea. However, the general is a meticulously honest and forthright man."

"But he has a preference. So do you."

"Of course."

"It helps that English Jack was the owner of a shanty hell."

"What are you implying?"

"Just wondering how magnanimous you would be feeling toward Rachel Bailey if she had shot Niles Keach, for instance."

Bracken's eyes narrowed. "I won't deceive you. I hardly think killing English Jack constitutes a criminal act."

"That's where you and I differ."

"So what will you do?"

Torn looked away. He was silent for a full minute. The normally impatient Bracken was discreetly patient this time. He could sense that Torn was fighting a tough inner struggle.

"I figured I'd let her go," Torn said eventually.

Bracken was surprised. "Not because of the telegram. You didn't know about that, did you?"

"I guessed it was coming. But no, not for that reason."

"Then why? She shot a man down in cold blood, didn't she? It was premeditated murder, wasn't it?"

"Trying to talk me out of it?"

"Certainly not."

"Good." Torn stood up. "By the way, how much has Mr. Thomas Bailey promised to donate to the Great Western?"

Bracken started to wax indignant. Then, suddenly, he relaxed and laughed. It was the one and only time Torn heard an honest-to-God laugh come out of the man.

CHAPTER 26

RACHEL BAILEY HAD BEEN HELD IN TORN'S PRIVATE Pullman. She was given the run of the place. An Irish Brigade man was on guard at all times, but was not to enter the Pullman under any circumstances. For his part, Torn had moved into the boxcar stables. He slept rolled up in a blanket on a pallet of hay, with a saddle for his pillow. It wasn't bad at all. He had known worse accommodations, and he had been on the frontier too long to need a bed for sleeping.

There was no jail in Sidewinder—no structure substantial enough to qualify. Moynihan was being detained in a freight car not far down the road, under guard. Recently Duffy and his associates in the Arroyo Grande business had been put in another freight car. Torn maintained it was still wise to keep Moynihan isolated from the others. Bracken was less than keen on the prospect of tying up two cars—

which otherwise could be engaged in hauling supplies to end-of-track—just to incarcerate a handful of criminals, but he indulged Torn.

After his meeting with the Great Western's superintendent, Torn went straight to his Pullman to tell Rachel Bailey she was free.

The news stunned her. She stared at him a moment as though she suspected this was some cruel jest.

"But . . . but I committed murder."

Torn nodded. "Yes, you did. How do you feel about that?"

"I wish I hadn't done it."

She said it contritely, sitting there in a wing chair, looking down at her hands, which were clasped tightly in her lap. Torn judged her remorse to be genuine. She was pale and looked haggard, and he figured she had to be going through hell. Taking another life, under any circumstances, was not easy to live with. But when it wasn't self-defense—when it was cold, calculated murder—that was a terrible burden for anyone who had even a shred of humanity.

Torn could sympathize. As a judge, he had sentenced men to death—men who had posed no direct threat to him. It made no difference that all the men he had sent to the gallows had been murderers. Condemning a man to death had bothered him from the very beginning of his career, and it still bothered him. That was one reason he preferred giving outlaws he hunted a fair chance. Not just because he thought they deserved it, but because it eased his conscience. The public didn't understand. They didn't bother to try. They censured him and his brand of justice. But he saw it in a different light, and he wasn't one to care much what people thought, anyway.

"I'm glad you feel that way," he told her. "If you didn't, I'd have second thoughts about releasing you."

"But why? Why are you letting me go?"

Torn shrugged. "Your father is pulling strings."

"My father?"

"He doesn't want to make the same mistake twice."

"He knows what I've done?"

"Probably read it in a newspaper."

"How can I possibly face him?" she cried. "I've disgraced him. The family. I—"

"You did what you thought you had to do."

"But it was wrong."

"Yeah. And you'll have to live with that."

"My father isn't the reason you're letting me go. There must be more to it."

"What does it matter?"

"You're simply not the kind of man who would bend to that kind of pressure."

Torn thought it over. "Miss Bailey, I'm not sure why. Maybe it's because every time I think about you on trial for murder, I picture your sister putting a pistol to her head."

Rachel tried to blink back the tears. But this time her composure shattered, and she wept bitterly, her hands covering her face, her body racked with sobs. Torn did not put a comforting arm around her trembling shoulders. He did not utter a consoling word. Instead he merely stood there and watched, impassive.

Eventually she cried it out, regained control of

herself. Dabbed at her red and bleary eyes with a lace handkerchief. She was so petite, so lovely, so ladylike, thought Torn, that it was still hard to believe she had literally blown English Jack Gellhorn's brains out.

"They say you've killed many men, Judge Torn," she said. "How do you . . . how do you come to terms with it?"

"I don't," he said bluntly. "I just live with it."

"But how?"

"If you got used to it, if killing comes easy, you cease to be a human being. You just . . . live with it. They will always come back to haunt you. Until the day you die, Miss Bailey."

She shuddered.

"You're free," he said. "There will be an eastbound out of here early in the morning. You will be provided with a pass signed by Orly Bracken so that you can ride the Great Western to the end of the line. I understand your father has arranged for your passage from that point on. I guess that about covers everything. So if there is nothing else . . ."

"The hunter," she said in a small voice. "Mr. Gant. Would you know . . . ?" She faltered.

"I have no idea," said Torn, shaking his head. "I reckon he's gone back up into the mountains."

"If only I had—"

"Forget it. Mark it down to a missed opportunity. In such things, you never get a second chance." His smile was bitter. "Believe me. I know."

He turned away, leaving the Pullman.

It was late, and Sidewinder was in full swing. So Torn strolled toward the noise and the action and the lights. He needed a drink. He happened to know that some of Gellhorn's bonded bourbon had found its way into the stock of a saloon called the White Elephant, and that the proprietor of that seedy dive had been blessed with sufficient wisdom not to water it down. There Torn bent his steps.

The shanty hell was busy. Irishmen were packed in shin by shoulder. Nonetheless Torn reached the bar with surprisingly little difficulty. The bartender knew him—knew also what he was after without needing to ask.

As he poured the shot of bourbon the apron said, "Stranger been in here asking about you."

"What about me?" Torn was distracted by thoughts of Melony Hancock and missed chances, and wondering why he couldn't take his own advice.

"Wanted to find you."

"Railroad man?"

"Naw."

"What did he look like?"

"Like a kid. Short, slight build. Wore a red shirt. Rattlesnake band on his hat. Big spurs. Kept ringing them against the boot rail. Guess he liked to hear 'em sing."

"Real polite?"

"Yeah. Now you mention it."

Torn felt an icy chill trickle down his spine.

"You know him?" queried the bartender.

"Yes," said Torn flatly. "The Cimarron Kid."

The barkeep's eyes widened. "You don't say? Why, he's supposed to be the fastest man with a gun alive today."

Torn nodded.

"That youngster—the Cimarron Kid?" The

barkeep shook his head in wonder. "He's a friend of yours?"

"Not exactly," said Torn. "In fact, I think he's been paid to kill me."

CHAPTER 27

TORN FINISHED HIS DRINK AND TRIED TO IGNORE THE barkeep, who moved on down the bar and began to spread the word around that the fastest gun on the frontier was here in Sidewinder and that he was gunning for the judge. Men glanced at Torn with curious pity, as though he were already dead and all they were waiting for was word on the funeral.

Leaving the saloon, Torn found small solace in the fact that the Cimarron Kid had a reputation for fair play. He had killed over a dozen men, but every one had been in a fair fight. So Torn didn't have to worry about getting back-shot, at least. Cold comfort, because he realized he didn't stand a chance in hell of coming out of a gunfight with the Cimarron Kid alive.

But Torn was not one to prolong the inevitable. He figured the best he could do was to make his pres-

ence conspicuously known in Sidewinder and let the
Kid find him. Then they could get it over with. He
couldn't run and he couldn't hide and he couldn't
break the rules and do something underhanded like
trying to get the drop on the Kid. He would just have
to hope for a miracle.

Collie Rourke found him before the Kid did.

"Word's out," said Collie. "A gunslick named the
Cimarron Kid is looking for you, Judge."

"So I've been told."

"Stinson's work?"

"Probably. English Jack warned me the colonel
was sending someone to clean my plow."

"English Jack warned you?"

"He wasn't all bad, Collie."

"So you knew this was coming."

"I didn't have any idea it would be the Kid. Just
proves it's a small world."

Collie squinted suspiciously. "You're sure cool
about it, Judge. You think you can beat this Kid to
the draw?"

Torn shook his head. "Not a chance."

"Sounds like you know him."

"We've met. Not too long ago, up Nebraska way.
The Kid was working for a man who tried to stir up
trouble between a rancher and some farmers in a
dispute over who owned a piece of land. That time
the Kid got away. I had a gut hunch we'd cross paths
again, though."

"What are you going to do?"

"Only thing I can do."

"Pride goes before a fall."

"I won't run, Collie."

"No. You canna run. But you canna commit flamin'

suicide, either. There's more than one way to skin a cat, you know."

"What's on your mind?"

"I'll get the Brigade together. We'll corner this shootist and deal with him in the best Irish tradition."

"Forget it," said Torn sternly. "God knows how many of your boys would eat lead. I don't want that on my conscience. The Kid came looking for me. It's my fight. You and the Brigade stay out of it."

Collie grimaced. "Well, it's been nice knowing you, Judge."

He walked away.

Torn continued on his way. He stuck to the middle of the street. This wasn't bravado. It simply provided him with a better view and improved his chances. He didn't want to turn a corner and run into the Kid face-to-face. This way he could keep some distance between them. Distance and darkness could only work to his advantage. And he needed any advantage he could come by honorably.

He watched the men going and coming out of the shanty hells on both sides of the street—and many of them watched him. The word had indeed spread, like wildfire, and these men knew there was liable to be a killing in Sidewinder before the night was done. Torn figured it wouldn't be long before the word reached the Cimarron Kid.

He was right.

A knot of Irishmen in front of a tent saloon parted hastily as a slight young man wearing a red double-breasted shirt and a matched pair of pistols emerged from the place. He stepped out into the street. Torn stopped. Thirty feet separated them, and that was close enough for Torn's liking. The Irishmen behind the Kid scattered. But elsewhere, up and down the street, other men were gathering to watch the spectacle of sudden death play itself out, willing to risk the stray bullet for firsthand experience of a shootout that had *famous* written all over it.

"Howdy, Judge," said the Kid.

"Hello, Kid."

"You make some powerful enemies."

"How much is Stinson paying you?"

"I'm sorry, sir," said the faultlessly polite and softspoken killer. "But that's privileged information. And by that I'm not saying I know anybody named Stinson, or that anybody paid me to do anything."

"You're not saying he didn't."

The Kid smiled. "I almost didn't come."

"Why not?"

"I don't want to kill you, sir."

"Then walk away."

"You know I can't do that. I walked away once before. And some folks have been talking about that. Can't have such talk getting around."

"So it's not the money. It's your reputation you're worried about."

"In my business, reputation is everything."

"Why did you walk away the first time? You knew gunning down a federal judge would make your reputation. Maybe it's because you knew it would also put a noose around your neck, sure as Christmas. I didn't think that would stop you, Kid. You're not interested in living to a ripe old age. You're the kind willing to die for glory."

"It isn't how you live, sir," explained the Kid. "It's how you die."

Torn shook his head. "I've heard that before. And as they lay dying they all change their minds."

"Then what are you doing here?"

"I don't aim to die, Kid. You got cold feet the first time, in Nebraska. What are you afraid of? Don't you know you're faster than me?"

"I'm also a better shot."

Torn hooked his frock coat behind the butt of his Colt Peacemaker. "Let's find out."

The Cimarron Kid slapped leather.

He stood against a backdrop of light spilling out of the door of the shanty hell from which he had just issued. Torn could see the Kid better than the Kid could see him. The Kid's hands streaked for the pistols in their cross-draw holsters faster than the eye could follow, but at the first sign of movement Torn was diving to his right, dropping to the ground. He was quick, but the Kid was a shade quicker. Torn felt the impact of a bullet—it felt like a sledgehammer striking him in the ribs. He fell, gasping for air, almost blacked out, but fought against it, rolling, dragging the Peacemaker out of his holster. The Kid kept shooting. His pistols boomed, spitting yellow blossoms of flame in the darkness. The bullets kicked dirt into Torn's face. Torn stopped rolling. On his belly, he aimed and fired. The Kid staggered, then dropped to his knees. Both his pistols discharged again, but this time they were aimed at the ground instead of Torn. Again Torn fired. Again his bullet found its mark, hurling the Cimarron Kid backward . . .

. . . As Collie Rourke pushed his way through the circle of men in the street, he saw the Kid sprawled on his back and Torn facedown in the dirt, and his first thought was that the two men had killed each other. He looked around him, at the grim, silent men. Not a word was spoken.

"Take those flamin' hats off," he growled. "The judge was a damn fine man, and he deserves a little flamin' respect."

Heads were bared. "The Kid was faster," someone said.

"Aye," said another. "But Judge Torn stood in there."

"Of course he did," said Collie. "That's the kind of man he was."

"Must've been Irish," someone murmured.

And then, with a groan, Torn rolled over and sat up.

"Jaysus!" gasped Collie.

He rushed forward, helped Torn to his feet. Torn was pale, his face etched with pain. He looked at Collie, and at the circle of astonished Irishmen, and smiled weakly.

"What is this? A wake?"

"How in the devil . . . ?" began Collie.

Torn held his frock coat open. He and Collie both could see it. The Kid's bullet had punched a hole in the leather sheath holding the saber-knife against Torn's rib cage. Torn pulled the saber-knife out of the rig. Two inches below the guard, the bullet had bent the steel of the blade.

"You *must* be Irish," Collie decided, awestruck. "Because you got the luck, for sure."

CHAPTER 28

THE NEXT MORNING FOUND TORN ENSCONCED ONCE more in his private Pullman. At dawn Rachel Bailey had caught an eastbound train, on her way back to Philadelphia and her father.

Torn was shaving when he heard horses outside. He put down his straight razor, wiped lather off his cheeks, and stepped out onto the vestibule to find Captain Buck Drayton and his five comrades-in-arms.

"Well, Captain," said Torn, "this is a surprise."

Torn had donned boots and trousers but wore no shirt, so Drayton's attention was drawn to the bandages encasing his chest in a tight dressing. "What happened to you?" he asked.

"Cracked rib."

"Hurts like hell, I guess."

"Considering the alternative, I'll take the cracked rib any day. What brings you?"

"We want to go home."

"Home?"

"Tennessee. But you still hold our parole."

"Where's the Whitworth, Captain?"

"We left it." Drayton glanced at his troops. "Truth is, Judge, we broke our word. We used the Whitworth once more."

Torn's gray eyes narrowed. "I've had no news. . . ."

"We blew up a bridge," said Drayton. "A Coastal and Northern bridge."

Torn was speechless.

Private Rosser grinned at the expression on Torn's face. "I told you, Cap'n. He don't believe it."

"When did this happen?" Torn asked.

"Yesterday," said Drayton. "They'll never beat you to Wolf Creek Pass now."

Torn's instincts told him that Drayton was telling the truth. The man had no reason to lie about such a thing. Besides that, Buck Drayton did not strike him as a man prone to lying.

"I don't understand," said Torn. "Why did you do it? Why the change of heart?"

"To set things right," Drayton replied gruffly. "Make amends. You were right, Judge. The war's over. After what happened with Sergeant Gregg, I could see it was so. I was fooling myself. We were nothing but mercenaries. Used the Cause as an excuse. But the Cause is lost. We talked it over. We're through fighting. We just want to go home."

"We spiked the Whitworth," said Rosser, a little sadly.

"Left our colors there, too," added Private Brown.

"Well, I'll be damned," Torn breathed. Then he thought about Ezra Stinson—and laughed. It was a short laugh—it hurt too much. Left him wheezing at the pain in his chest.

"That was . . . an honorable act," he said.

Drayton shook his head. "No. We could have surrendered with honor thirteen years ago. Everything we've done since then has been without honor."

"What's done is done. Put it behind you. Go home, and good luck to you all."

Drayton saluted, wheeled his horse around, and rode away, followed by the others.

Torn was watching them go as Niles Keach walked up. Keach was grinning ear to ear.

"We made it," he crowed. "We reached Wolf Creek Pass. We beat the Coastal and Northern, Judge."

"Yeah, I know," said Torn.

Because he realized that the destruction of a bridge would have brought the Coastal & Northern to a screeching halt. Drayton's Light Horse Artillery had delivered a death blow to Stinson's railroad.

"You know?" Keach asked. "How is that? We just got word from end-of-track."

Torn made no reply. Brow furrowed, Keach looked beyond Torn at the six riders headed east along the iron road.

"Who were those men?" he asked.

"Good soldiers," replied Torn, and turned to go back inside the Pullman.

"I almost forgot," said Keach, pulling Torn's saber-knife from under his coat. "Picked this up from the smitty for you, Judge. Good as new."

Torn took the saber-knife, nodding his thanks.

"Reckon it's over?" asked Keach. "Reckon Stinson will try to take the pass from us?"

"He might try," Torn said grimly, fierce determination flashing in his gray eyes. "But he'll fail."

As Torn disappeared inside the Pullman Niles Keach nodded, smiling confidently.

He figured with Clay Torn on their side, they couldn't lose.

HarperPaperbacks *By Mail*

If you like Westerns, you'll love these...

8 WESTERN CLASSICS

THE GLORY TRAIL
by Mike Blakely... Few men
have a bigger dream than
Texas Ranger Lawnce
McCrary to make Texas a
land of peace.

DIRK'S RUN
by Paul Garrisen...Dirk
wasn't running from
danger—he was riding
toward death

VENDETTA GOLD
by Mike Blakely...
author of "The Glory
Trail"—Before Roy Huckaby
can find the hidden treasure,
he must first help settle a
bloody family land war

TEXAS DRIVE *by Bill Dugan*...
in the lawless west, you
either pack a gun—or die!

DIRK'S REVENGE
by Paul Garrisen...
Dirk was a gun for hire—and
a man marked for death.

SPIRIT'S GOLD
by Stuart Dillon...
He'll risk his life to find a
beautiful woman's hidden
fortune in gold.

**GUN PLAY AT CROSS
CREEK** *by Bill Dugan*...
Morgan Atwater can't run
from the past—he has to
settle in blood!

DUEL ON THE MESA
by Bill Dugan...
After his family is massacred, Dalton Chance wants
nothing except Indian blood!

**...from today's best selling Western authors.
Authors like Mike Blakely, Paul Garrisen,
Bill Dugan, Stuart Dillon.**

**Visa and MasterCard holders—call
1-800-562-6182 for fastest service!**

MAIL TO:
**Harper Paperbacks, 120 Brighton Road
PO Box 5069, Clifton, NJ 07015-5069**

Yes, please send me the Western Classics I have checked:
| | The Glory Trail (0-06-100013-2) $3.50
| | Dirk's Run (0-06-100035-3) $3.50
| | Vendetta Gold (0-06-100014-0) $3.50
| | Texas Drive (0-06-100032-9) $3.50
| | Dirk's Revenge (0-06-100035-3) $3.50
| | Spirit's Gold (0-06-100054-X) $3.95
| | Gun Play at Cross Creek (0-06-100079-5) $3.50
| | Duel at The Mesa (0-06-100033-7) $3.50

SUBTOTAL .... $_____

POSTAGE AND HANDLING* .... $_____

SALES TAX (NJ, NY, PA residents) ...... $_____

TOTAL: $_____
(Remit in US funds do not send cash)

Name_____

Address_____

City_____

State_____Zip_____
Allow up to 6 weeks delivery
Prices subject to change

*Add $1 postage handling for up to 3 books
FREE postage/handling if you buy 4 or more.

HP-004

Saddle-up to these

THE REGULATOR by *Dale Colter*
Sam Slater, blood brother of the Apache
and a cunning bounty-hunter, is out to
collect the big price on the heads of the
murderous Pauley gang. He'll give them
a single choice: surrender and live, or go
for your sixgun.

THE REGULATOR—Diablo At Daybreak
by Dale Colter
The Governor wants the blood of the
Apache murderers who ravaged his
daughter. He gives Sam Slater a choice:
work for him, or face a noose. Now
Slater must hunt down the deadly rene-
gade Chacon…Slater's Apache brother.

THE JUDGE by *Hank Edwards*
Federal Judge Clay Torn is more than a
judge—sometimes he has to be the jury
and the executioner. Torn pits himself
against the most violent and ruthless
man in Kansas, a battle whose final ver-
dict will judge one man right…and one
man dead.

THE JUDGE—War Clouds
by Hank Edwards
Judge Clay Torn rides into Dakota where
the Cheyenne are painting for war and
the army is shining steel and loading
lead. If war breaks out, someone is
going to make a pile of money on a river
of blood.

🔲 HarperPaperbacks *By Mail*

5 great westerns!

THE RANGER *by Dan Mason*
Texas Ranger Lex Cranshaw is
after a killer whose weapon
isn't a gun, but a deadly noose.
Cranshaw has vowed to stop at
nothing to exact justice for the victims, whose numbers are still
growing…but the next number up
could be his own.

Here are 5 Western adventure tales that are as big as all
outdoors! You'll thrill to the
action and Western-style justice: swift, exciting, and man-
to-man!

Buy 4 or more and save!
When you buy 4 or more
books, the postage and handling is FREE!

**VISA and MasterCard holders—call
1-800-331-3761
for fastest service!**

MAIL TO: Harper Collins Publishers, P. O. Box 588, Dunmore, PA 18512-0588, Tel: (800) 331-3761

YES, send me the Western
novels I've checked:

☐ **The Regulator**
0-06-100100-7 . . . . $3.50

☐ **The Regulator/
Diablo At Daybreak**
0-06-100140-6 . . . . $3.50

☐ **The Judge**
0-06-100072-8 . . $3.50

☐ **The Judge/War Clouds**
0-06-100131-7 . . . . $3.50

☐ **The Ranger**
0-06-100110-4 . . . . $3.50

SUBTOTAL . . . . $_____

POSTAGE AND HANDLING* . . . . $_____

SALES TAX (NJ, NY, PA residents) . . . . $_____

Remit in US funds,
do not send cash   **TOTAL: $_____**

Name_____

Address_____

City_____

State_____Zip_____ Allow up to 6 weeks delivery.
                                Prices subject to change.

Add $1 postage/handling for up to 3 books…
FREE postage/handling if you buy 4 or more.

H0131

If you enjoyed the
Zane Grey book you have just read…

GET THESE 8 GREAT

Harper Paperbacks brings you Zane Grey,

THE RAINBOW TRAIL.
Shefford rides a perilous
trail to a small stone house
near Red Lake, where a new
enemy awaits him—and an
Indian girl leads him on a
dangerous adventure toward
Paradise Valley and his
explosive destiny.

THE DUDE RANGER. Green-
horn Ernest Selby inherits a
sprawling Arizona ranch
that's in big trouble. Pitted
against the crooked ranch
manager and his ruthless
band of outlaws, Selby is
sure bullets will fly.…

THE BORDER LEGION.
Roving outlaws led by the
notorious Kells kidnap an
innocent young bride and
hold her in their frightening
grasp. Thus begins a wave of
crime that could be stopped
only by a member of their
own vicious legion of death.

THE MAN OF THE FOREST.
Milt Dale wanders alone
amid the timbered ridges
and dark forests of the White
Mountains. One night, he
stumbles upon a frightening
plot that drives him from his
beloved wilderness with a
dire warning and an inspir-
ing message.

THE LOST WAGON TRAIN.
Tough Civil War survivor
Stephen Latch will never be
the same again. Emerged
from the bloodshed a bitter
man, a brigand with a ready
gun, he joins a raging Indian
chief on a mission of terrify-
ing revenge—to massacre a
pioneer train of 160 wagons.
But fate has a big surprise!

WILDFIRE. Wildfire is a legend, a fiery red stallion who
is captured and broken by
horse trainer Lin Stone. A
glorious beast, a miracle,
Wildfire is also a curse—a
horse who could run like the
wind and who could also
spill the blood of those who
love him most.

HarperPaperbacks *By Mail*

ZANE GREY WESTERNS

the greatest chronicler of the American West!

SUNSET PASS. Six years ago Trueman Rock killed a man in Wagontongue. Now he's back and in trouble again. But this time it's the whole valley's trouble—killing trouble—and only Rock's blazing six-gun can stop it.

30,000 ON THE HOOF. Logan Huett, former scout for General Crook on his campaign into Apache territory, carries his innocent new bride off to a life in a lonely canyon where human and animal predators threaten his dream of raising a strong family and a magnificent herd.

Zane Grey is a true legend. His best selling novels have thrilled generations of readers with heart-and-guts characters, hard shooting action, and high-plains panoramas. Zane Grey is the genuine article, the real spirit of the Old West.

Buy 4 or More and $ave

When you buy 4 or more books from Harper Paperbacks, the Postage and Handling is **FREE**.

MAIL TO: **Harper Collins Publishers**
P. O. Box 588, Dunmore, PA 18512-0588
Telephone: (800) 331-3761
Visa and MasterCard holders—call
1-800-331-3761 for fastest service!

Yes, please send me the Zane Grey Western adventures I have checked:

- ☐ The Rainbow Trail (0-06-100080-9) $3.50
- ☐ The Dude Ranger (0-06-100055-8) $3.50
- ☐ The Lost Wagon Train (0-06-100064-7) $3.50
- ☐ Wildfire (0-06-100081-7) $3.50
- ☐ The Man Of The Forest (0-06-100082-5) $3.50
- ☐ The Border Legion (0-06-100083-3) $3.50
- ☐ Sunset Pass (0-06-100084-1) $3.50
- ☐ 30,000 On The Hoof (0-06-100085-X) $3.50

SUBTOTAL . . . .$_____

POSTAGE AND HANDLING* . . . .$_____

SALES TAX (NJ, NY, PA residents) . . . .$_____

               TOTAL: **$_____**
(Remit in US funds, do not send cash.)

Name_____

Address_____

City_____

State_____ Zip_____
Allow up to 6 weeks delivery.
Prices subject to change.

*Add $1 postage/handling for up to 3 books…
  FREE postage/handling if you buy 4 or more.

H0011

HP-001-12 11 10 9 8 7 6 5 4 3 2 1